"Come here, Rachel." The command was very soft.

She wanted  She really wanted take her in his hurt. But that wo she thought, and

"Why not?" he asked gently. "You once told me you were scared of no man. I only want to hold you, to wipe away your tears."

"There are no tears to wipe away, Alex," she said, lifting her face to him. "See, the tears you saw the other night were the last. There won't be any more."

"Oh, Rachel, you're trying to be so strong, so tough," he murmured hoarsely. "You're so tough that all I've been able to think about is holding you and feeling your velvet skin beneath my fingers." His arm curved around her before she could respond, and he led her over to the sofa. "Listen to me Rachel. All of us, no matter how tough, sometimes need someone to hold onto. Hold on to me for awhile."

What he said touched her deeply, and she murmured "You?" The tears she said were gone forever appeared in her eyes. "You're too hard, Alex."

"Yes, I am, and that means I have more than enough strength for both of us. Come here, Rachel . . ."

WHAT ARE *LOVESWEPT* ROMANCES?

They are stories of true romance and touching emotion. We believe those two very important ingredients are constants in our highly sensual and very believable stories in the *LOVESWEPT* line. Our goal is to give you, the reader, stories of consistently high quality that may sometimes make you laugh, sometimes make you cry, but are always fresh and creative and contain many delightful surprises within their pages.

Most romance fans read an enormous number of books. Those they truly love, they keep. Others may be traded with friends and soon forgotten. We hope that each *LOVESWEPT* romance will be a treasure—a "keeper." We will always try to publish

*LOVE STORIES YOU'LL NEVER FORGET
BY AUTHORS YOU'LL ALWAYS REMEMBER*

The Editors

LOVESWEPT® • 107

Fayrene Preston
Rachel's Confession

BANTAM BOOKS
TORONTO • NEW YORK • LONDON • SYDNEY • AUCKLAND

RACHEL'S CONFESSION
A Bantam Book / September 1985

*LOVESWEPT® and the wave device are registered
trademarks of Bantam Books, Inc. Registered in U.S. Patent
and Trademark Office and elsewhere.*

ISBN 0-553-21699-6

Published simultaneously in the United States and Canada

---

*Bantam Books are published by Bantam Books, Inc. Its
trademark, consisting of the words "Bantam Books" and
the portrayal of a rooster, is Registered in U.S. Patent and
Trademark Office and in other countries. Marca Registrada.
Bantam Books, Inc., 666 Fifth Avenue, New York, New
York 10103.*

PRINTED IN THE UNITED STATES OF AMERICA

O   0 9 8 7 6 5 4 3 2 1

My thanks to Pam and John Renner,
whose enthusiasm and love of Florida
helped me immensely.

One

The Florida night was wild. Thunder rumbled overhead and slashes of incandescent silver light flashed in the dark, angry sky. Out on the St. Johns River the wind was whipping up white-tipped waves. Along the bank the Spanish moss writhed in a frenzied dance as the wind whooshed through the branches of the oaks and cypresses, making a plaintive kind of music of its own. According to the local weatherman there was a hurricane hovering out in the Atlantic, and if it kept on its present course, it would hit the Cypress Cove area in approximately forty-eight hours.

Alex Doral stood in the shadows of the white clapboard Yacht Club enjoying the untamed elements around him. The air had a quality about it that was palpable, almost as if he could reach out and take hold of big chunks of it. One side of his mouth lifted in a smile that held more than its share of cynicism as the thought crossed his mind that the threatening storm was infinitely more entertaining than the dance he had just left. With one notable exception, that is, he mused.

Alex stuck a slim brown cheroot between his teeth. Twisting to face the building, he hunched his broad shoulders and cupped his hand around his lighter as he lit the cheroot and inhaled deeply. "Yacht Club." What a farce. He would venture a guess that for most of the illustrious members adventure and sailing meant sitting on the decks of their boats at sunset and toasting the position of the sun over the yardarm.

He didn't even know why he had bothered coming tonight. He supposed it was because someone had told him that it would be a good opportunity to meet some of the people of the community on a social level. He had been bored, so he had decided to go along with it—until he had arrived and realized he had no desire to know any of the people there.

Except for the woman called Rachel. Inside the ballroom he had barely been able to take his eyes off her, a predicament he had noticed that he shared with the majority of the men present.

She had been on the dance floor most of the night, the major portion of it with a sandy-haired man. Alex had disliked him on sight. He had a preppie look, the look of one born to wealth. Alex knew that look well; people he had grown up with had it.

But Alex had been able to detect immediately in the sandy-haired man's face elements of weakness and dissipation. His talent of acute observation had been honed under fire; and as the evening had progressed, his observation proved out, for the man had gotten steadily drunker. The woman called Rachel hadn't seemed to mind, however. Nor had the men who had been queuing up to dance with her.

She had twirled and swayed around the dance floor with first one man and then another. Tossing her shining length of chestnut-brown hair, she had moved her hips and feet in time to the throbbing beat of the music, seemingly oblivious to her surroundings. And in a rush of amber chiffon her skirt had whirled up around her thighs, showing provocative glimpses of long, slender legs. She had hypnotized, she had tantalized.

She had been like a flame, undulating in the minds of all the men who saw her, making them burn for her. And Alex had been no exception. But he had never been the type of man to stand in line for anything, especially for a woman. So he had left. There would be another time, of that he was sure.

Looking down at the rows of slips, he saw sleek white sailboats and gleaming cruisers straining at their moorings. Extra fenders bobbed in the churning black river, their taut lines secured to the bow rails. The corklike fenders cushioned the bows of the boats against the dock. Idly he wondered if the storm would come close enough to test the strength of this old building's hurricane shutters. Not that it concerned him one way or the other. He had sat out hurricanes here and there, and he had discovered that if one had adequate shelter, ample provisions, and charming company, a hurricane could be quite an entertaining experience.

Charming company. Once more his thoughts went to the woman called Rachel. To have her, alone. . . . He flicked his cheroot into the night and tried to decide if he should go back inside and say good-bye to his host or simply disappear into the night as he wanted to do. Almost immediately he decided on the latter. He had never been one for social conventions and he couldn't think of a good reason to begin to conform to them now.

Rachel pushed her fingers through her hair, holding it off her damp forehead for a moment. Up on the bandstand the musicians were blasting out the latest dance number, and all around her dancers were responding. Until now she had enjoyed the party. The people, the champagne, the music— they helped blot out things better forgotten. But suddenly, it was as if someone had changed the lighting, brought in new people, raised the volume of the noise level. Instead of working for her, her surroundings had begun to work against her, and she knew that she couldn't dance one more dance without getting away by herself for a time.

"Come on, Rachel. How about dancing this one with me?"

She swiveled and met the laughing gaze of Scott Roberts. "I think I'm going to sit this one out. Thanks, anyway." He was the fourth man she had turned down in as many minutes.

He grabbed for her arm and began persuasively pulling her onto the floor. "Aw, come on, honey. The dance floor won't be the same without you."

"*No!*" She wrenched her arm out of his, wishing that her date would come back. But the question of where Sean was didn't cross her mind.

She knew she probably had to look only as far as the bar to find him.

What kind of husband was he going to be if he continued to drink as much as he did? she wondered. As always when that particular question arose in her mind, Rachel attempted to dismiss it. And as always it didn't work. There were no two ways about it. She hated that Sean drank too much. She had had a prime example of what drink could do to a man in her father. And the thought that she might be repeating her mother's mistake scared her to death.

She had certainly tried to get Sean to lay off the booze since they had started dating. He made lavish promises to her and usually managed to break them all within days. Just like all men, Rachel thought. The condemnation flicked contemptuously through her mind.

She frowned at the route her thoughts had taken. It seemed to be getting harder and harder to control them, and that wasn't a good sign. Get tough, Rachel! You'll never get what you want by being squeamish. And in the end it won't matter, she said silently to herself for perhaps the hundredth time. As long as Sean gives you access to his bulging bank balance, nothing else will be important. She reached out a gleaming bare arm and grabbed a glass of champagne off a silver tray being passed by a waiter. Taking a sip, she frowned again. It tasted strangely bitter.

"Rachel, Rachel . . . don't be mad," Scott was begging engagingly.

"I'm not, really," she reassured, feeling a stab of guilt that she had totally forgotten he was standing there. Her head was beginning to hurt, and she could feel the tenuous hold she had on her composure beginning to slip away. Handing Scott her glass with what she hoped was a smile, she tried to concentrate on him. Well-dressed and attractive, he was one of the up-and-coming young business-men of Cypress Cove. Just because at present he wasn't in the league that she wanted to play in didn't mean he never would be. Besides, she liked him. She tried to think of a way to pacify him yet get rid of him at the same time. "Scott, I'm a little tired right now and I need to take a break. Ask me later in the evening."

His face brightened. "You got it! See you later, honey."

"Right, sure." Rachel scanned the room for the nearest exit.

Her need to escape was reaching a desperation point. In this sea of people she felt alone. The loud music had become a solid wall, moving in on her, and the stinging smoke felt like a blanket lowering to cover her, smother her. Pressing fingers to her aching temple, she glanced wildly around for Sean. She located him—a ludicrous sight—trying to do the limbo underneath one of the tables the caterers had set up. Just as she had feared, it wasn't even midnight yet and he was already drunk out of his mind. She turned away disgusted. He obviously wouldn't miss her.

The band had started a stirring, yet sentimen-tal number, and lights threw colored streamers over the crowd, casting an eerie illumination. Without a backward glance Rachel escaped onto the darkened, windswept veranda and thrust her shoulder against the frame of the French door, sighing in deep relief as she did so. She could still hear the music, only now it was muted, more bear-able. And she would have a few minutes alone. She knew no one else would venture out on a night like this.

As she made her way to the edge of the veranda the wind came at her immediately, pulling at her hair until the chestnut-brown strands were a tousled mass, flowing around her head. Rachel didn't care. She breathed in the fresh air, desperately needing to be revitalized.

She would have laughed at herself if she hadn't felt so disturbed. In spite of her strong resolve to go after all that life had to offer, there were moments like this that would sneak up on her. Moments of weakness when she would remember and feel she couldn't go on. Moments of vulnerability when she felt as if she were about to break apart. Moments that were more frequent than she would like to admit.

The wind slid over her skin, cool with a hint of dampness to it. It caught at the chiffon skirt of her dress, tossing the amber material about her knees, playing with it.

The band was doing a selection of songs from the *Let's Dance* album. The lead singer didn't have that haunting, compelling quality to his voice that David Bowie did, Rachel thought. Still, the lyrics spoke to her, especially when he sang of running and hiding. What would it be like just to be able to take off and run through the cool black night until she couldn't run anymore? Then maybe lie down on some thick, grassy lawn and sleep until her cares were no more.

Alex stood without motion, a trick that had saved his life more than once in the jungles of Central and South America. A pale-gold sweep of light spread across the veranda from the closed doors, reaching to the woman called Rachel. She was so

still. He would have thought her a statue if he
hadn't seen for himself the way she had scintil-
lated and swayed on the dance floor, her dress
floating out in rippling waves around her, poetic
and provocative.

Just then a vicious clap of thunder resounded,
but she didn't even flinch. His interest deepened.
This was an entirely different woman from the one
he had seen inside, dancing, laughing. Apparently
there was turmoil within her that was equal to or
greater than the impending storm around her.

Rachel grasped the balustrade, still turning
the song's lyrics over in her mind. Running away
wouldn't work. Neither would sleeping for a long,
long time. She knew she would eventually have to
wake up, and when she did, she would find that
everything was the same.

When would it stop, this terrible, wrenching,
emotional pain? Unconsciously she crossed her
hands over her stomach. She had been home for
months, and there were times when she was sure
she would feel no more pain. Then it would happen
suddenly, catching her unawares, and the pain in
her heart would be so intense that it would
threaten to overwhelm her.

She lifted her eyes to the sky. As black as the
night was, it was filled with all sorts of light. There
were the fog lights along the pier that cast out over
the river, picking up the colors in the iridescent
foam of the whitecaps. There were the strings of
fairy lights in the trees around the club, shimmering like a thousand stars in the wind. And there
was the brilliant white fire of the lightning, tearing
through the clouds, illuminating, then dissolving,
leaving the clouds a deep navy-blue.

Her mind went back ten months to another

night. That night hadn't been this decorative. No, then there had only been rain, so much rain that it had seemed to come down in solid sheets. And blackness. Terrible, endless blackness. That night ten months ago in Atlanta when her baby had died.

Behind her she could still hear the music. She lifted her face into the wind, barely aware of the tear that spilled down her cheek, followed by another, then another.

Her tears were totally unexpected to him. And somehow a bit unnerving—tears running down the flawless skin of the glittering creature who, just minutes before, had dazzled all who had seen her on the dance floor.

She heard only the wind over the muted music, so she had no warning of his approach. But all at once there was a sudden warmth down one side of her, a remarkable lessening of the wind against that side, and the very sure sensation that he was standing beside her. Slowly she turned, to a man who seemed to have been born out of the lightning and the thunder of the dark and violent night.

Her eyes. They were the color of sherry and by rights should be soft and warm. Instead they were without light and extraordinarily sad. He reached a long brown finger to her face, taking a glistening teardrop onto it and saying, "A beautiful woman and tears are against the laws of nature."

It was only then that she realized she had been crying. Appalled that anyone should catch her at such a vulnerable moment, Rachel brushed the back of her hand over her cheek and fought to regain her composure. "And you, of course, Mr. Doral, are an expert on beautiful women."

"You know who I am?"

He was tall with straight black hair that was blowing in the wind. His face was angular with strong cheekbones and a hard jawline. His brows were thick and dark, and over the left one a scar was slashed through the smooth golden-brown skin to his temple. It was his eyes, however, that really riveted her. Aquamarine, like the jewel. With his white dinner jacket and dark pants, his dark hair and light eyes were a devastating combination. But then she knew his background—an American father and a Latin-American mother, diplomats for the United States government.

"Of course," she replied, answering his question evenly. "Alejandro Doral, adventurer, tycoon, and ladies' man. You've been the topic of conversation in Cypress Cove for weeks now, Mr. Doral. Pictures of you have been in our paper. No one old enough to read or listen to gossip could help but know who you are." She saw his eyes narrow and realized that she had managed to disconcert him in some way. Something that probably didn't happen often. "And by the way," she added softly, "no one knows more about tears than a beautiful woman."

Alex regarded her thoughtfully. If he had caught her in an unguarded moment before, that moment was definitely over now. She was back to being the cool beauty he had watched earlier. The beauty who appeared so confident of her powers and who knew so well how to use them. His next words were calculated. "But it's such a waste. Instead of tears, you should be wearing diamonds."

She gave a bare sound of a laugh, and Alex found himself bending forward to try to catch the sound. But it was picked up and carried away by the wind, leaving behind the sensation that it had teased him.

"Something else you're an expert on, too, I understand. Diamonds. It's common knowledge that you own diamond mines."

She had said that as if she really couldn't care less, one way or the other, and was not at all impressed. Her eyes had gone back to the river, and Alex had the feeling his presence beside her was having very little impact on her. Just as the impending storm was. Her mind was elsewhere, and he didn't like it.

"You know a lot about me, but I know nothing about you. For instance, I know your first name is Rachel. But I don't know your last."

That drew her attention back to him. "How do you know my name?"

"The men who wanted to dance with you. They would call out your name."

Turning her back on the river, she leaned against the balustrade with her elbows resting casually on top of it. The wind flattened the dress against her, molding it to the shape of her, but she appeared unaware of the sensational effect of it. She inclined her head toward the wide doors. "You were in there? I had heard you would be here tonight, but I didn't see you."

"And you obviously weren't looking for me either," he remarked wryly. His eyes lowered to the wide strips of amber chiffon that covered her breasts. With her arms back, the cloth was pulled tightly across their fullness, and even though the material was lined, he suddenly imagined that he could see the rigid imprint of her nipples against the dress. The surge of heat that followed surprised him. These days a man rarely had to imagine. With the braless trend the outline of a woman's nipples beneath her clothes was an ordinary sight. Particularly in the crowd he ran with. Therefore, he mused, it was rather odd that something only imagined on this woman could excite him when so many times the blatant reality left him cold.

"Should I have been looking for you?"

"A lot of people were," he commented derisively. "But you . . . I had the feeling you weren't seeing much. Most of the time not even the man you were dancing with."

She turned her head back to him, controlling her annoyance. He was right, but she would almost bet her life that no one else had been able to detect it. And it irritated her to no end that this man, a stranger to their town, an outsider, had been able to. "You realize that those people in there are afraid of you, don't you?"

"Yes," he said simply. "And they should be."

The wind had not grown cooler, yet she shivered. The rumors were true, then. He was just as hard and tough a man as everyone said. Cypress Cove might survive a hurricane, but could they survive him? she wondered.

Without speaking, Alex peeled off his coat and placed it around her shoulders. The warmth from his body was still clinging to the jacket and it seeped into her skin. A smell she would almost describe as dark and wild and definitely musky floated into her senses. *This is the scent I would smell if he were holding me in his arms,* she thought unexpectedly, and shivered again.

His hands came to her shoulders. "You're cold. Let me take you home."

"No." She shook her head, and the wind flung

silky strands of reddish brown over his jacket and onto his hands. His fingers wrapped around a length of the hair.

"Why not?" The question was asked mildly, but Rachel had the feeling there was steel behind it. "You're as tired of this party as I am."

She didn't bother denying it, but she shook her head, dislodging the hair from his fingers. Her instincts were telling her it would be better if this man didn't touch her. "I have a date somewhere. Sean Dillingham." She glanced through the French doors but could see Sean nowhere. She hoped he hadn't passed out. Taking off the white jacket, she held it out to Alex.

He accepted it, but suggested, "Why not keep it on for a while longer?"

His shirt was startlingly white and fine across the broad width of his chest, and he didn't appear at all affected by the wind. Still, she had no intention of keeping his jacket on. It seemed too personal a gesture to accept from a man she judged as quite remote. "Because I'm not cold."

"Then if you didn't shiver because you were cold, you must have shivered because you, too, are afraid of me." Without having a definite accent, he had a way of speaking that was faintly foreign and, if one were not careful, virtually spellbinding.

Her sherry-colored eyes turned solemn, fascinating him. "No, Mr. Doral, I'm not afraid of you. Although, now that I think about it, I suppose I should be." Despite her statement she shrugged with a motion that bespoke utter indifference. "You've inherited a paper mill that in a town of ten thousand employs two thousand. Whatever you decide to do about the mill will have a critical effect on this town's economy. Your decision can't help but affect me and every person in this town, however indirectly. But rest assured, I'm not afraid of you or any man. Not any more. Now, if you'll excuse me, I really need to go find out what has happened to my date."

"Wait a minute!" He grabbed her arm and turned her back to him. "You can't say something like that to me and then leave without explaining."

"I'm afraid I can, Mr. Doral," she pointed out softly, looking down at his hand on her arm as if it were particularly abhorrent.

"So you can, Rachel," he said, realizing with a start that the beautiful woman standing before him was so cool and in control now, that if he hadn't seen her tears for himself, he wouldn't have believed them. *Intrigued* was much too mild a word to describe what she was making him feel. That she hadn't tried to intrigue him only doubled the power of the impact she was having on him. "But you haven't told me your last name yet."

"It's Kirkland."

"Rachel Kirkland," he repeated, then smiled. "Please call me Alex. All my friends do."

She tilted her head, observing the way the shadows seemed to settle beneath his cheekbones, structuring his face into chiseled stone. "Alex." It was her turn to voice his name. She wasn't certain that she didn't like his full name of Alejandro better. Somehow it seemed a softer name than Alex. Alejandro. It was a name that could be murmured in answer to a gentle smile, a name that could be whispered in the darkness, a name that could be sighed in passion.

She pulled her thoughts up short. In the long run what did it matter? It was very unlikely that they would ever become friends—the powerful owner of the paper mill and a lowly bank teller. Besides, he wouldn't be staying in town long. Cypress Cove had nothing to offer a man who was reputed to inhale adventure and danger as casually as most men inhaled the fragrance of their after-shave lotion each day.

"Alex," she said again. "I think I better go find my date before he gets any drunker."

"You're not thinking of letting him drive you home?"

"I don't know." She sighed, all at once feeling very tired. "I'll figure something out. But there's really nothing to worry about. I can handle Sean."

Alex found himself inexplicably irritated. "I'm not so sure about that. He might insist on driving, and as drunk as he is, it would be extremely dangerous, especially on a night like this." He scowled. "What in the hell are you doing on a date with a fool like that anyway?"

She didn't disagree with his assessment of Sean. Slanting her eyes toward the ballroom, she said very slowly, very clearly, very flatly, "I'm going to marry him."

"Marry?"

She pushed away an errant strand of hair that had blown across her eyes. "Why not? He's not so bad when he's sober. And he's rich."

"Rich? A man's being rich is important to you?"

"Very," she stated without emotion, apology, or explanation.

Alex had never had a woman admit to him that she was after a man for his money, even when he had known for sure that she was, and he was almost struck speechless. Almost. He recovered quickly. His teeth shone very strong and white as he smiled. "Then there's no problem. I'm more than certain that I can buy and sell your date a hundred times over. Let's go."

For the first time she showed some emotion, however slight. "I can't leave him in there," she protested. "It wouldn't be right."

"Rachel, in the state he was in the last time I saw him, I don't think he's going to be aware of anything until morning. They'll let him sleep here tonight."

She cast another glance over Alex's shoulder at the sky just as a jagged silver streak stabbed through the clouds. Under normal circumstances she knew it would be better not to accept a ride home with Alejandro Doral. But for tonight at least, she decided she might as well be practical. "I suppose you're right," she admitted grudgingly. "And I'd hate to walk home in this. It hasn't started raining yet, but you never know."

"Then come on." His hand curled around her upper arm so that his fingers grasped the under-side of her arm and brushed the material that cov-ered the side of her breast. She couldn't be certain whether he'd intended it to happen, but whether he did or didn't, she still felt a warm melting sensa-tion.

In reaction she pulled quickly away from him. "I need to go pick up my purse."

"Do it," he instructed shortly. "I'll wait here for you."

Two

Alex's car was luxurious and had the potential for great power, but he drove it with firm control, guiding it through the tempestuous night. The weather wasn't really so bad yet. Still, even though he had been in far worse, seen far worse, he could understand why the people of Cypress Cove might be concerned. He knew if the storm did come inland, it had the potential for great destruction. But he had a feeling the hurricane would veer off.

Out of the corner of his eyes he observed Rachel and tried to decide if she was worried about the chance of a hurricane. Or, he wondered, did it disturb her to be so close to him, driving through the night? Somehow he thought the answer, at least to the last question, was no. She sat quietly, her hands resting atop a thin gold purse, her attention on the night outside the car. He didn't even think she realized that her fragrance was fill-

17

ing the car. Speculating on what it was, he idly ran down his repertoire of perfumes. He couldn't decide. He had never smelled anything that light, that romantic, that . . . *erotic*. Could it possibly be the way her skin smelled naturally? No, impossible.

Still, he would love to run his tongue over that smooth satin skin of hers to find out if she tasted like she smelled. Just thinking about doing it made heat rush to his loins.

He tightened his hands on the wheel. "Don't you think you should tell me where you live?"

"I'm sorry!" She glanced around with a startled look on her face. "In a small town everyone automatically knows where everyone else lives. I guess I forgot that you're new here."

He flexed his hand, then again took a tight grip on the wheel. "That's something you seem to be able to do rather easily—forget about me."

Surprised at his remark, she ran a hand through her disheveled hair and laughed huskily. "How could anyone forget about you, Mr. Doral?"

"People usually don't," he agreed tersely, angry with himself. He supposed he was so used to women going all out to win him over that he was letting it get to him that this woman obviously was not only *not* interested in gaining his attention, she was not at all impressed with him. "Are you going to tell me where you live?" he asked, once more glancing at her. He saw her put a hand briefly to her forehead, as if to say *How stupid of me*, and he felt a twinge of admiration. In his life he had found that honesty, in any form, was rare. But Rachel Kirkland seemed to have it in abundance, with at least a touch of self-deprecation added in.

"Of course," she said. "As a matter of fact, you and I are neighbors."

"Neighbors?"

"In a manner of speaking," she amended, laughing that wonderfully husky laugh of hers again that made him want to see if he could capture it with his mouth. "My grandmother's place is the next house after your estate on River Drive. The only thing is, your house sits on acres, and ours sits on just a patch of land and isn't the least bit grand."

"I think I know the place," he said, and fell silent.

He was an unusual man, Rachel mused, turning her attention back to the side window of the car. And his effect on the town would be fascinating to watch. She had been truthful with him. The fact that his stay in Cypress Cove might affect her directly really hadn't occurred to her before tonight. But now she let her mind wander over the possibilities. And strangely enough, her thoughts went to the personal repercussions rather than the financial.

Just being in an enclosed car with him was an exciting experience, Rachel thought. His charismatic personality was evident even when he was not speaking. He was a larger-than-life personality, an international businessman, a multimillionaire, the stuff that legends were made of.

Even though a plethora of words had been written about him, portions of his life remained shrouded in mystery. There were rumors, of course. The word *mercenary* had been used more than once in conjunction with the revolution-torn Central American country of Montaraz. And there were other, equally ugly things said about him. The only part of his life that he didn't seem reticent to speak of in the press were his love affairs. She, who normally didn't follow gossip columns, had seen countless pictures of him with one lady after the other on his arm. His women were always glamorous, always smiling, and always *clinging* to his arm.

There was no doubt about it. The man was exciting. But Rachel wouldn't allow his excitement to touch her. She *couldn't*. She had done that once—allowed a man's excitement to affect her. Only when it was too late had she discovered that it hadn't been excitement after all. It had been deception. And it had nearly destroyed her. Now she had a plan for her life. And nothing was going to deter her from it.

"Is that your house?"

"What?" She jerked her head around, realizing that they were already at her grandmother's. "Yes. Just pull in the driveway there." She indicated the dirt path that served as the driveway.

He pulled the car to a stop and switched off the engine. Wind swirled around them, but the car was big and heavy and took the buffeting well. Outside, thunder could be heard and lightning still flashed, but there was a certain security Rachel found to being inside the car. Or was it that she was with Alejandro Doral, who had the reputation of being able to handle any situation, anywhere, anytime? Could he handle a hurricane? she wondered.

"You said this is your grandmother's place." He nodded toward the two-story frame house.

Rachel followed his gaze. The house was small, really only one room deep and two rooms wide, and built on concrete blocks that were hidden by carefully tended camellia bushes. Discounting the apartment she had lived in for five years in Atlanta, it was the only home she had even known.

"Yes. My sister—Jaime—and I live there with her."

"With your parents?"

"No. Just Gran and ourselves. I had better be getting in. Thanks for the ride home."

"Wait." He put his hand on her shoulder. "Have dinner with me tomorrow night."

"No."

He swiveled in his seat, perplexed with himself because he was so reluctant to let her go, and perplexed with her, because she was so close, yet so distant. Almost in protest to her remoteness, he reached his fingers to her hair, absently noticing that he liked the way it seemed to pour through his fingers. "Why not?"

"My sister and I always reserve Sundays for our grandmother," she returned, realizing this was the second time tonight he had taken her hair into his hands.

Alex felt her stiffen and felt a compelling need to touch her, to stroke his hands over her, and to release the tenseness he could sense in her body. He wanted to know her, he realized suddenly—all of her, inside and out.

Softly he murmured, "Rachel, what is it? What's wrong? You have the color of fire in your hair." His hand slid slowly and with infinite sensuality down the smoothness of her neck to the bare slope of her breast and finally on to the gossamer amber chiffon that was covering her. "And there is the color of fire in your dress." His voice was deliberately quiet, flowing toward her, attempting to wrap her with its warmth. But she wasn't looking at him, and he couldn't be sure he had her attention. Grasping her chin in his hand, he turned her to face him. "So tell me, Rachel Kirkland, why is it that there is no fire in your eyes?"

Her breath had ceased its normal pattern at the same time his hand had begun touching her. Now she forced herself to regain control. She allowed no one outside her family to question her so intimately, and Alejandro Doral would be no exception. "You're an extraordinary man, Alex, who has found himself in an unextraordinary town for a short period of time. I'm sure you'd like some amusement, some woman to keep you company while you're here. You saw most of the available women at the party tonight and obviously you weren't impressed. Nevertheless, I must tell you I won't be the one to amuse you."

"Why not?" His hand had found the skin at the back of her neck underneath her hair and was rubbing. It was as soft as a child's.

"I have other plans for my life."

"Oh, that's right," he returned sardonically. "How could I have forgotten? Sean, the drunk. I'm sure you'll have a wonderful life with him." He brushed his hand to the side of her neck. He had discovered that Rachel Kirkland was infinitely touchable, and he couldn't seem to stop.

"Sean may not seem much in your eyes," she answered a trifle breathlessly, "but he is going to give me everything I want in life."

"Does he know this?" he demanded.

"He hasn't officially asked me to marry him yet, if that's what you mean, but it's only a matter of time."

"Does he know that you only want to marry him for his money?"

"He knows. I've told him."

"And what is his reaction?"

"He laughs," she scoffed disparagingly, "and he doesn't even have the sense to realize just how truly awful what I'm doing is."

He stared at her for a long moment, wishing he could see inside her mind. "What do you want, Rachel?"

Right at this moment, with his hand on her bare skin, Rachel couldn't have said what it was that she wanted. She hadn't forgotten exactly. It was just that there were other things that had suddenly required all her attention. Like the way her clamoring body was reacting to his hands.

"What do you want, Rachel?" he repeated. "Money?"

She found her breath. "Yes."

The pulse beneath his fingers was racing. Alex knew he affected her.

"Jewels?"

"Yes."

And he knew he affected her by the way her skin seemed to quiver beneath his hand. He also knew it by the nervous yet provocative way she was licking her lips.

"A position in society?"

She nodded.

He knew her skin would heat like satin on fire when he ran his hands over her.

"Security?"

"Yes." She could barely speak now.

He knew her mouth would open when he kissed her, and he knew his tongue would find unending sweetness.

"Love?"

She said nothing.

He knew he was going to have to kiss her very soon.

"Love?" he asked again.

"Is there such a thing?" she questioned with a breathy huskiness. "I'm not sure. Are you?"

"No," he admitted quietly, "even though love is what a lot of people spend a lifetime searching for."

"Not me. I refuse to waste my life searching for something that's just not there."

He paused. "What about passion?"

She looked at him. "I'm not sure that exists either."

He was silent for a moment. Then: "Come here, Rachel."

He drew her across his lap, folding her scented, silken length to him. He took his time, because he had been wanting to do this since he had first seen her on the dance floor. Like a flame, she had been. He would make her flame now. The music had moved her then. He would move her now.

Rachel felt dazed. It was as if it were all happening in slow motion. She saw it coming but couldn't stop it.

Alejandro Doral. She could feel his strength as he brought her to him, adjusting her body to his. She could feel his gentleness as he smoothed her tangled hair back from her face. Amazing. Too amazing. She began to struggle.

But his lips came down and softly touched the place on her cheek where his finger had taken the teardrop. Then they moved on, to the other cheek, where his tongue gave a tiny lick. She calmed in his arms. Lifting her hair away, he found the hollow behind her ear, staying there, just letting his mouth rest on the beating pulse and breathing in that unique perfumed scent of her.

Feeling hot and weak at the same time, Rachel protested, "I've got to go in."

In silent answer his arms tightened and his lips moved to her mouth and took possession. Sure and sweet, they brushed back and forth, sensitizing her to their subtle pressure until his tongue flicked out, seeking entry. Without consciously making the decision, Rachel opened her mouth to his, receiving the thrust of his tongue. It was madness, she thought. It was all madness. Her heart seemed to be beating with the force of the thunder around them.

Lord, but she was sweet, Alex thought, listening to the small sounds she made in the back of her throat, feeling the way she practically melted into him. In a way it was more than he had expected. In another way it wasn't nearly enough. His hand dipped beneath her dress to clasp one tantalizingly rounded breast.

Suddenly she pushed against him, fighting for breath. She brushed her hand across her eyes, then looked away from him toward the small two-story house that was her home. Focusing on the house helped give her the perspective she so desperately needed. It stood between two live oaks and for an instant appeared in relief against the blackness, outlined by a bold streak of lightning. The house was close to one hundred fifty years old and seemed too fragile to withstand a storm of hurricane force, but it had withstood many such storms. And so would she. "I've got to go in," she insisted. With a murmur of chiffon she slid off his lap and away from him. "Thank you for the ride home," she said politely. Then thrusting open the car door, she ran, stopping only to open the small gate in the picket fence.

With a strange smile on his face Alex watched her run across the wide yard in a froth of chiffon and flying hair. She had gotten away from him tonight, but he knew there would be another time. He was a master strategist, and there wasn't a doubt in his mind that the woman called Rachel would be in his arms again. Soon.

Three

Rachel awoke to the sound of a steady rainfall outside her window. The hurricane had changed its course during the night, and the wind had followed. Thank God. Their budget wouldn't stretch to house repairs caused by the damage from a hurricane—or anything else, for that matter. She rolled over on her back and glanced at the other bed. Jaime was already up. It must be later than she thought.

Her eyes focused on the white alarm clock next to her bed. Eleven o'clock! She was sure she had set the alarm for seven.

A closer inspection of the clock proved her right. Either Gran or Jaime must have turned it off, and Rachel had to admit that it was just as well. Even with sleeping until eleven, she hadn't gotten a lot of sleep. Tossing and turning for what seemed like hours, her body had felt as full of restless emotions as the night outside, while her thoughts had been entangled with Alejandro Doral. In her mind the man, his kisses, and the storm had somehow all become one. It wasn't until the storm had begun to abate toward morning that she had slept.

Still, that didn't excuse her. She had wanted to get up early and help Gran finish sewing Jaime's school wardrobe—if you could call such a meager amount of clothes for a teenager a wardrobe. Jaime never complained, but Rachel ached to give her sister all the beautiful clothes she herself had never had when she had been growing up. Luckily Gran had passed her sewing skills on to her, though admittedly she didn't love sewing as her grandmother did. But she was thankful she had the ability. It enabled them all to have better clothes than they might normally have had.

Money. It had been the bane of her existence for as long as she could remember. There never seemed to be enough. Jaime needed braces, and Rachel had been trying to put aside a little money every month for that purpose, but on her small salary as a bank teller it was definitely tough. Her job in Atlanta as a model had paid much more. Her dream had been to work her way up to buyer, and it would have happened, except . . .

Dreams had a way of dissolving like sugar in a rain, and that part of her life was over. She couldn't allow herself to think about it. She had no more dreams. Now she only had plans. And those plans hinged on marrying Sean Dillingham.

Sean, with his blond hair permed to just the right amount of chic curliness; his rather Adonis appearance; his happy-go-lucky personality; his penchant for designer labels; his little-boy smile.

On their first date he had told her he wanted her. On their third date he had said he loved her. Soon he would realize that she meant it when she said she wouldn't go to bed with a man unless she was married to him.

It was a rule she was not about to give in on. On this she was firm. Never again would a man have her without marrying her. Never again would she be used by a man. From now on she would be the user. She was the one who would be in control.

She was only twenty-five, but she felt she had the experience of a woman twice her age. And she owed it all to David. David with the beautiful eyes and the pretty talk. David with his promises, his caresses—his betrayal. Rachel blinked back the tears that were threatening. *No more tears,* she told herself.

Once she and Sean were married, there would be no need to scrimp. Jaime could have her braces. And she would redo Gran's house for her, not just redecorating either. As old as the house was, it needed lots of renovation. The plumbing needed to be replaced, and the house completely rewired. Then there was the new roof. It all required money.

Her mind returned to Sean. She hoped he wouldn't kick up a fuss because she had let someone else take her home. It was the first time she had ever done such a thing to him. But then again it was the first time he had ever been that drunk. Even if Alex hadn't offered to drive her home, she would have asked someone else to.

Alejandro Doral. The man with the jewel colored eyes and the strangely heated lips. He had seen her crying, something she hadn't even allowed Gran or Jaime to see. He had driven her home and kissed her.

In the distance she heard the phone ring. It rang twice before someone picked it up.

"Rachel!" She could hear Jaime bounding up the wooden staircase. Jaime never walked, and she never sat still. At twelve, almost thirteen years of age, she was a whirlwind of frenetic energy. "Rachel!" Jaime stuck her head in the doorway. Her red hair, as usual, sprang in thick washboard waves about her head. As beautiful as Jaime's hair was, somehow it never looked tidy unless she took the time to braid it. And time seemed a rare commodity for Jaime. She had never known a bored day in her life. She was always busy, and she had a natural enthusiasm for life that drew people to her.

Her green eyes shone with a teasing light as she looked at her big sister. "Pretty Boy Sean is on the phone. I told him I wasn't sure you could come to the phone. How about I tell him to call back in a couple of years?"

"And how about I wring that pretty little neck of yours?" Rachel sprang out of bed, pausing long enough to grab her robe from the foot of the bed. "Jaime, you're going to have to learn to be more polite to Sean. After all, he's going to be your brother-in-law."

"Not if there's any justice in the world!"

"Jaime Brooke Kirkland, you're incorrigible!"

Hurrying barefoot down the stairs, Rachel's forehead pleated into a frown. It worried her that Jaime disliked Sean, and that Gran wasn't exactly happy about him either. They were the two most important people in the whole world to her, and it really mattered to her that they approved of both Sean and her plan to marry him. Especially since it was as much for them as it was for herself that she was going to do it. Halting at the bottom of the

staircase, she reached over the railing for the phone. It was on a table that sat to the side of the stairs.

"Hello?"

"Rachel. Are you still speaking to me?" Sean's words were thick and slow.

Ah, good, she thought. He was feeling bad and uncertain about her reaction to his behavior the night before. This wasn't going to be so hard after all. "Of course, Sean. How are you feeling?"

She heard him groan and smothered a smile.

"I've felt better. What happened? I woke up in one of the guest rooms here at the Yacht Club, and you were nowhere to be found."

"Surely you didn't expect me to be there with you?" She infused definite shock into her question.

"Maybe I didn't expect it, but it sure would have been nice." It was a familiar theme of his, trying to get her into bed. "How did you get home?"

"I got a ride with some friends. I just didn't feel it would be safe to let you drive me home, Sean," she said seriously. "I was a little disappointed in you."

"Lord, I'm sorry, Rachel. I guess I got carried away with the drinks. It's just so damn frustrating, wanting you and not being able to have you."

"Don't blame this on me, Sean."

"Well, it's the truth," he muttered sullenly. "But I promise it won't happen again. Forgive me?"

She didn't answer right away, letting him think she was having a tough time making the decision. "I suppose. But you know my main concern is for you." On certain levels that was true.

Sean was twenty-seven and in many ways still a boy. It was time he grew up. "I worry about you."

"You do?" His voice lightened a fraction. "Listen, honey. I've got to go home and make peace with Mom and Dad, but how about I come over tonight? We can go somewhere."

Rachel winced at the thought of his parents. They didn't approve of her, and it was probably why he hadn't asked her to marry him yet. His father was a real-estate developer, and Rachel had the impression they felt she was only out for their money. That they were right didn't matter, she rationalized. Sean was crazy about her. He wanted what she could give him physically. She wanted what he could give her materially. It would be an even trade.

"No, Sean. You know I can't accept dates on Sundays."

"Then Monday. How about Monday night?"

She hesitated. It might do him good if she played hard to get for a little while. Maybe it would straighten him up and lead him to ask her to marry him. "I'm busy for the next few days, Sean, but I'm sure I'll see you around."

"Well . . . can I at least call you?"

"Of course, Sean. Feel better. Bye." She replaced the phone and glanced over her shoulder. Jaime was nowhere to be seen. Maybe she was upstairs making their beds. Rachel smiled to herself. For all Jaime's prickly teenage ways, she was a good girl. But Rachel could foresee that the next few years were going to be hard on all of them. Money would make it easier. She would see to it.

She made her way around the stairs and into the room they used as a casual living area, searching for Gran. The room was empty, but she stopped anyway, her mind taking in the familiarity of the room, imagining how money could improve it. She grinned as she admitted to herself that Gran might not let her do much, even if she had the money. The room was neat, cheerfully faded, and, most important, designed with a decor of the heart—her grandmother's heart. From the scarf-covered table in the corner ladened with family photographs, to the sofa—which was the first piece of furniture she and Rachel's grandfather ever bought—the room spoke of the history of her grandmother's life. The old sofa had been recovered many times over the years and sorely needed it again. But it would have to wait, just like everything else.

Rachel passed under the molded archway, past the dining room, and into the kitchen. The kitchen had formerly been the back porch and ran three quarters of the way across the back of the house. As she expected, she found her grandmother seated in the little breakfast nook, her silver head bent over a hem she was sewing on a skirt for Jaime. Although she seemed much too thin for Rachel's liking, she was a striking woman, even now when she was nearly seventy. When she had been a young girl, her hair had been as beautiful a shade of red as Jaime's. Jaime had inherited the full color from Gran; Rachel had received only a red tint.

"Morning, Gran. I told you I would help you with Jaime's school clothes today. Why didn't you wait for me?"

"You haven't looked well since you've been home. You need your sleep."

"Something that wouldn't hurt you either, you know," she returned wryly. For as long as she could remember, her grandmother had risen at five A.M. with dependable regularity, whether it was a weekday, a weekend, or a holiday.

"When you get to be as old as I am, you don't need that much sleep." She set aside the skirt and glanced out the window. "The weatherman reported that the hurricane veered off in the night."

"Good. All we'll get now is a good rain." Rachel reached for a cup and poured herself some coffee.

"How was the dance last night, dear?"

"Fine, I suppose, although Sean got drunk." She didn't want to go into her spell of panic that had overtaken her in the middle of the party. After all, it had passed.

"You didn't let him drive you home, did you?" The alarm in her grandmother's voice brought her mind back to the kitchen.

"No, I didn't," she reassured, sorry now that she had brought the subject up. "And I wish you wouldn't worry about me."

"But I do. You've changed so much since you came home from Atlanta. You've become positively . . . fragile."

"*Fragile!*" Rachel sat down beside her grandmother and took her hand in hers. "Gran, I'm all grown-up now, and I know what I want out of life and exactly how to get it. Don't worry about me. I've never been stronger."

Gran frowned. "The really worrisome thing is, you believe that. But the truth of the matter is that you're as fragile as one of my old pieces of china—extremely brittle and about ready to crack."

Rachel sat back with a perplexed look on her face, unable to understand why Gran would say such a thing. She opened her mouth, but just then

Jaime flew through the door. "For the sake of our house I'm glad the hurricane decided not to come this way. But still, you have to admit, it would have been exciting. I've never seen a hurricane."

"And with luck, you never will, child. Now, sit down and let me cook you some breakfast."

"Or better yet, Gran," Rachel offered, "you sit still, and Jaime and I will cook yours."

"I ate hours ago."

"Then sit there and talk to us while we cook for ourselves. Okay, Jaime?"

"Sure," her young sister returned cheerfully, already rummaging in the refrigerator for the eggs.

"So who brought you home, Rachel?" Her grandmother had resumed her sewing.

"This you won't believe. None other than Alex Doral himself."

"Wow!" Jaime turned from the refrigerator so quickly, she almost dropped the eggs in her hand. "Now that's what I call excitement. Is he as gorgeous in person as he is in the newspapers?"

"Gorgeous?" Rachel thought about it. No, he was too rugged to be called gorgeous. And there was too much strength of character in his face. And that scar. . . .

"Earth to Rachel. Earth to Rachel."

"What?" she asked blankly.

"Is he a hunk or isn't he?"

Rachel laughed in spite of herself. "Yes, I suppose you could call him a hunk."

"My friends are just going to flip out when I tell them he brought you home!" Jaime emphasized her words by dramatically plunking down the carton of eggs.

All humor left her voice. "Well, then don't tell them."

"Aw, Rachel."

"I mean it, Jaime. He was just doing me a favor, and I'm sure that's the last time I'll see the man. I don't know about him, but I sure don't want a lot of rumors starting up about the two of us. And this town is just capable of doing that very thing."

"All right." Jaime grinned and held up her hands in a gesture of surrender. "But if you ask me, it's a darn shame."

"Nobody asked you, Jaime."

The day passed pleasantly. Gran did some baking, while Rachel started the special dress she was making for Jaime to wear to her thirteenth birthday party. Supper was a light one, consisting of the week's leftovers.

Around nine o'clock the phone rang. Rachel answered, "Hello?"

"Have you had a good day?"

Alejandro Doral. She recognized his voice immediately, but why was he calling? Rachel wondered. "It's been very nice," she answered. "And yours?"

"Boring."

So much for pleasantries, Rachel thought wryly. "May I ask why you're calling?"

"I want you to have dinner with me tomorrow night."

Dinner? Rachel instantly came to the conclusion that dinner—or anything else for that matter—with Alex Doral was out of the question. Totally impossible. She knew there were a lot of ways she could handle the situation, but she decided to be straight with him. There was no sense in playing coy. Not with this man. He was much too dangerous. "Look, Alex, this is all very flattering, but I'm afraid I'm just not interested."

"Not interested," he repeated thoughtfully. "Well, then, do you think you might be interested the day after tomorrow?"

"No."

"Next week?"

"No."

Silence stretched to her over the line. "I gave you tonight, Rachel. I'm not giving you another night."

"What?" Rachel didn't know whether to laugh or be angry. She laughed. "You may be a powerful man, Mr. Doral, but even you can't give people nights. Tonight was mine to do with as I pleased. I did."

"I gave you tonight, Rachel." His voice was deliberately soft and husky. "Tomorrow night is mine. Good-bye."

Alex hung up the phone and smiled to himself as he thought of the astonished expression that must be on Rachel's face. Leaning back in the big chair, he reached for his lighter and set it to a slim cheroot. Only after he had exhaled a long stream of smoke did he shift his eyes across the room to where Rand Bennett was sitting. "The lady turned me down."

"So I gather." A look of extreme amusement creased the features of Rand's handsome face. "This town can't be as bad as you've made it out to be, Alex, if a woman who lives here actually had the good taste to turn you down. I must meet her."

"Oh, you will," Alex returned confidently. "But that's all you'll do. This one is mine."

Rand spread his hands in a gesture that was meant to convey total innocence. "Since when have I ever interfered with your love life?"

Alex viewed affectionately the man who had

been his friend since college. At one time they had been very much alike, doing everything together. When he had made the decision to go to Montaraz, Rand had gone with him. But Rand had left early; Alex had stayed on until it was too late. They were no longer alike, but they were still the best of friends.

In answer to Rand's tongue-in-cheek question, he enumerated, "Well, let's see, there was that time in Rio, for one. What was her name? Ila? And then how about that time in Montevideo?"

The permanent lines beside Rand's eyes deepened as he laughed. Something he did a lot of. "That was Margarita."

"Right, and let's not forget Juanita in Santiago."

"Doesn't count, and you know it. Those women weren't important to you. This one is apparently different. She's obviously gotten under your skin."

"You're right about that." Alex exhaled a stream of smoke out of the side of his mouth. "It's the damnedest thing I've ever run into, Rand. I can't figure her out. The first time I saw her, she was all fire and grace, moving across the dance floor like a living dream that seduces. The next time I saw her she was standing on the veranda like an ivory statue, weeping, surrounded by a storm that was making no impact on her. Then"—his hands went out in incomprehension—"a few minutes later she was telling me, in a rather detached, indifferent way, that she intends to marry for money."

Rand's eyebrows rose, almost disappearing beneath his thick brown hair. "And she's not interested in *you*? She obviously doesn't know who you are, then."

"She knows," Alex said softly. "And she's still not interested. I get the feeling that somehow I just don't fit into her plans."

"So what are you going to do?"

Alex smiled. "Change her plans."

The next person in line stepped up to the window and handed Rachel her deposit. She rolled her shoulders imperceptibly. She had been working steadily since nine this morning and she could feel the tension in her shoulders and neck. Counting other people's money was a tedious, exacting job, and it required total concentration. And it was boring. So boring.

After graduation from high school, she had worked in the Cypress Cove Bank for a year to get enough money to go to Atlanta. The fact that she had had previous experience as a teller in the bank should have made it easy for her to get a job when she had moved back to town. But Mr. Sifferman, the bank manager, had looked on her with suspicion. Because she had "flitted off to the big city" once, she might do it again, he had said. In the end he relented, but only after a stern lecture on loyalty and "stick-to-it-iveness," plus a reminder that she would be on probation. These last few months Rachel had had to work extra hard to prove herself. And on top of the other strains in her life she knew it was beginning to tell on her.

"Have a good day." Rachel bade good-bye to the lady with the absurdly large picture hat and dipped her head to her cash drawer.

A moment later she raised her head and smiled automatically. "May I help you?"

Alejandro Doral drawled, "I'm sure you can." And her smile froze.

Rachel glanced quickly around. Dammit! She was the only teller on duty at the moment. The other teller was on a break. She would have to deal with Alex herself. "I wasn't aware that you had an account with us."

"I needed an auxillary account to expedite my business here. My main banking is done through New York."

"Of course." A man like Alejandro Doral would probably have a hundred accounts scattered around the world, Rachel mused. "So what can I do for you?" she asked, wishing there was some other way she could phrase the question.

He smiled, and the smile traveled across his lips and down her spine. "You can have dinner with me."

"I told you that I wasn't interested in having dinner with you."

"Rachel, Rachel," he murmured in a tone that sounded troublingly intimate within the austere confines of the bank. "What have you ever heard about me, or what have I done, to lead you to believe that I would take no for an answer?"

Her lips moved, but she was unable to form a reply to such an extraordinary question. Behind him people were shuffling impatiently in line, waiting their turn. And she could feel Mr. Sifferman's eyes boring into her back. She could almost hear his disapproval, as if he had shouted it across the library-quiet atmosphere of the bank. *What do you mean by delaying an important man like Alejandro Doral?*

"Do you have any business you wish to conduct here today, Mr. Doral?" she questioned from between clenched teeth.

"I'm conducting it."

"Mr. Doral!" Mr. Sifferman, suddenly at Alex's side, was beaming, and began pumping his hand enthusiastically. "How nice to see you today, but you must know that you don't have to stand in line. I'll be most happy to handle any of your transactions *personally*."

"That's not necessary, but thank you anyway. I'm sure Ms. Kirkland will most graciously help me."

"Well, of course, she will!" Mr. Sifferman glared at her with barely concealed animosity. "Immediately! I'll get Tina back to take over at the next window and that way we'll get these people taken care of quicker." He hustled away to pull the unsuspecting Tina off her break ten minutes early.

"Are you satisfied?" Rachel hissed.

"Not yet. Will you have dinner with me tonight?"

"Will you leave if I say yes?"

"Yes. And by the way, we won't be alone. I have a friend staying with me."

She tried to hide her surprise. "Am I supposed to be reassured by a friend of yours?"

"You will be once you meet him. You'll like him. He's a doctor." He gave her an infuriatingly pleasant smile. "The only person I know more trustworthy than a doctor would be a priest. Personally I don't know a priest, but if you do, you're welcome to invite him."

"You're impossible!"

"Actually I'm easy, but we'll discuss that later. Will seven-thirty be all right for me to pick you up?"

"I suppose," she muttered ungraciously. "But don't pick me up," she added. "I'll walk over. I enjoy walks in the evening."

"Really?" he asked as he turned to leave. "That's interesting. For a woman so determined to marry for money, I thought at the very least you would demand a limo."

"What exactly is it that you have against this man?" Gran questioned. She was sitting comfortably in a padded rocking chair, watching as Rachel discarded first one dress and then another as inappropriate to wear for dinner.

Rachel turned to look at her grandmother. The rocking chair had been in that very spot for as long as Rachel could remember. Gran had told her that she and Jaime had been rocked in it and that she was saving it for her great-grandchildren. The thought of holding a baby in her arms, rocking it to sleep, caused Rachel's forehead to crease in reaction to the familiar pain that wouldn't go away.

"Rachel?"

"Nothing, really," Rachel finally conceded, returning her attention to the limited contents of her closet. Why should what she was going to wear tonight be bothering her so? It wasn't as though she had that much to chose from. "I don't have anything against Alex. It's just that he makes me nervous." She pulled a garment from the closet, looked at it, then thrust it back. Temporarily giving up, she went to sit on her bed. "No, that's not right. I'm not exactly nervous around him. It's more as if I feel I should be . . . *careful* whenever I'm around him."

"Careful?"

Rachel grinned. "Careful. You know, as in, Look both ways before you cross the road or you might get hit by a semi."

"So you equate Alex Doral with an eighteen-wheeler." Her grandmother considered the idea. "He must be a very interesting man."

"Believe me, he lives up to all his advance publicity—and then some. You should have seen him in the bank today. Mr. Sifferman was practically drooling at the sight of him. And although the people behind him were definitely getting restless, they didn't dare say a word. They knew who he was and how much the future of this town depends on him."

Suddenly Gran set the chair rocking vigorously back and forth and shook her head. "What's going to become of you, Rachel?"

It alarmed her to see that worried look on her grandmother's face. "Gran, even if Mr. Doral shuts down the mill, we'll be all right. If the worst happens and I lose my job at the bank, I'll go up to Jacksonville and get a job. I'd hate leaving you and Jaime again, but I'd do it, and at least I'd be close enough that I could come home on weekends. Don't worry about Alex Doral."

"I'm worried about *you*, Rachel. Not the mill or this town. I worry about your future. Your relationship with David left you so scarred. How are you ever going to find happiness?"

Rachel sank down in front of her grandmother, taking her hand in hers. "Now, you listen here. I will not have you upset, do you hear me? I'm going to be fine. We're all going to be fine. My future will be taken care of. Sean is going to give me everything I've ever wanted, and you and Jaime too. I'm going to be happy."

"You don't believe that. You can't. You know I've never spoken ill of your father to either you or Jaime, but I think now is the time to say it. He was an alcoholic. He stayed with your mother because she was his strength and he was smart enough to know it. But she couldn't remain strong. All the work and worry got her down. Then she became pregnant with Jaime and grew so frail. She didn't have the strength to live through the delivery, and your father couldn't handle it. He packed up and left. A month later we got the news that he had been killed in a drunk-driving accident, some floozy beside him. It was only by God's grace that no one else was killed. But there you were, a motherless child, all of thirteen. And Jaime, a newborn baby. No mother, no father."

"We had you, Gran," Rachel soothed, "and we've done just fine."

"You're like your mother, Rachel. Inside you have a beautiful and innocent sensitivity. Too much so. You barely survived David. You'll never be able to endure what living with Sean will do to you."

"You've got to stop this worrying! It's not good for you and I don't like to see it. I know all you say about my father is true. But there's a difference between Sean and him. Through his family, Sean has access to a lot of money."

"Humph!" Gran snorted. "What kind of man doesn't even earn his own living? Sean is weak."

"It's true, he is," she admitted. "But it's just as well. It makes it easier for me to handle him."

"You mark my words"—Gran shook a warning

finger in her face—"you're never going to be happy with a man you can handle, Rachel."

"Happiness is relative, Gran," she replied sadly. "I've at least learned that much."

She walked through the evening shadows, approaching the great Spanish mansion through the piny woods. It sat on a slight rise, surrounded by splendid oaks, with an emerald-green lawn sloping down to the river. Palms swayed over the red-tiled roof and ivy climbed over the arches.

Rachel stopped and surveyed the house. Although she had lived next to it most of her life, she had never been inside. Alex's aunt had been a rather eccentric old lady. When she wasn't traveling the world, she had stayed to herself, giving little thought either to her neighbors or to the mill that she owned. The mill had been her husband's, and while he was alive, it had thrived. Now, though, it was common knowledge that it showed the neglect that it had received at Alex's aunt's hands. By contrast the house had always been kept up, and Rachel couldn't deny the natural curiosity she had about it.

But now Alex lived there. He had invited her to dinner, and she didn't have to question his motives for asking. He was new to town, without a woman, and—did her heartbeat really pick up at the thought?—attracted to her. She still retained the vivid memory of his kisses. They had caused an unfamiliar movement somewhere deep within her. She couldn't allow that to happen again.

As for her motives for accepting Alex's dinner invitation, she told herself they were relatively simple. He had put her on the spot at the bank, and she desperately needed to keep the job until she and Sean were married. And that would be soon. She would see to it.

But first she had to get through the evening with Alejandro Doral. It would be exciting, that much was for sure. And dangerous. An uneasy thought occurred to her right before she set out across the lawn: Could one really walk through an evening of fire and expect to come out on the other side of it alive or even unscorched?

Four

Rachel lifted the heavy brass knocker and let it fall. A moment later Alex opened the door. Although he was casually dressed in a gray turtleneck sweater and black pants, a sexual potency easily equal in effect to the storm of two nights before was radiating from him.

He smiled and extended his hand, and almost against her will she took it. "Come in, Rachel. You look very beautiful." His hand wrapped around hers with what felt to be a warm, welcoming pressure, but still Rachel knew she couldn't afford to relax. His aquamarine eyes were sharp and more glittering and dangerous than ever.

The large room he led her into struck her as odd at first. Her impression was that everything fit, but that it shouldn't have. Chinese, Jacobean, Spanish, and English Tudor furniture mingled comfortably with one another, their massive proportions looking exactly right in the room. There were satin draperies and silk chairs and velvet-covered couches. Priceless objets d'art were artfully arranged, and paintings of wild animals and birds mixed with seventeenth- and eighteenth-century originals and hung almost ceiling to floor on beige suede-covered walls. The room was unusual and exotic, like the man who now owned it.

It was a bit much to take in at one glance, so it wasn't any wonder that at first she missed the man reclining in the wing chair by the crackling fire.

He was a slender, elegant man with thick brown hair that feathered down across his forehead in a careless fashion and an extremely pleased expression on his handsome face. Rising, he approached her. "You must be the incomparable Rachel." Taking her hand from Alex's without a flicker of apology and heedless of the instant scowl it put on his friend's face, he pulled her to a small couch. "I'm so glad to meet you. I'm Rand Bennett and we're going to be the best of friends."

"We are?" Rachel asked faintly. Then, as his name registered she added, "You *are*?"

"I are what? Would you like a drink?"

"No, thank you. You are Dr. Rand Bennett? I've heard of you."

"Uh-oh." Rand grinned at Alex. "I'm in trouble."

"I wish," Alex muttered, although he was viewing his houseguest with a good-humored expression on his face. "You know as well as I do that the press paints you only in the most glowing of terms."

"He's right," Rachel exclaimed. "Practically every heart surgery you perform in Houston makes front-page news with your innovations." She decided not to add that the Houston socialites he squired around town garnered an almost equal share of space.

"You're exaggerating," Rand said unaffectedly, "but if it impresses you, pretty lady, then that's all I ask in life."

"You're being outrageous, Rand," Alex murmured. "Give Rachel a chance to breathe."

Alex had put his finger on the problem, Rachel thought a bit dazedly. Being in this fantastic room with two such forceful, charismatic men left little space for breathing. She wasn't prepared. Her simple sweater and skirt in autumn colors, which seemed so casually chic in her bedroom mirror, now left her feeling exposed, unprotected, and out of place.

"Are you sure you won't have a drink, Rachel?" Alex asked, clearly attempting to put her at ease.

"A club soda, please." She would need all her wits about her tonight, trying to hold her own with these two men, she told herself. Alex's next question proved her point.

"Did your boyfriend's drunken behavior the other night put you off drinking?"

"I've never drunk much." Having an alcoholic parent sort of puts one off drink, she thought grimly. Except, of course, for the other night. If she remembered correctly, she had had quite a bit of champagne. But then that stormy night had been an exception to just about everything, she mused, recalling Alex's kisses and her response.

"I see." He smiled and changed the subject. Dislodging Rand's hand from Rachel's, he handed her the club soda. "Don't worry. I won't let Rand bother you too much, and I'll send him to the guest house directly after dinner."

"I eat slowly," Rand informed Rachel with a twinkle in his eyes, "and you're just as beautiful as Alex said. Tell me all about yourself."

Taking a sip of the club soda, Rachel watched Alex as he leaned against the fireplace. He appeared to be interested in the fire as he kicked a log into position with one boot-clad foot, but somehow she knew his attention was totally focused on her. It made her wary, and she opted for an easy yet honest way out. "I never talk about myself. It's too boring a topic. I'd much rather hear about you, Rand."

"A woman who doesn't like to talk about herself." Rand's eyes widened in admiration. "You *are* different, but then Alex said you were."

Rachel was beginning to wonder what else Alex had said about her when a dark-skinned, white-coated man entered the room. "Dinner." The one word was spoken with a thick Spanish accent.

"Thank you, Carlos." Alex forestalled Rand by reaching for Rachel's hand and pulling her to her feet. Tucking her hand into his arm, he began to lead her toward the dining room. "I hope you like the dinner Carlos planned."

Not to be outdone by his friend, Rand latched on to Rachel's other arm. "Yes, despite the fact that he was born in Montaraz, Carlos is a very continental cook."

Montaraz. There was the name of that country again. Could the rumors about Alex possibly be correct? Could this urbane, sophisticated man have been a mercenary? She waited until Alex had seated her and situated himself at the head of the table before saying, "Rand mentioned Montaraz, Alex. Have you ever been there?" She saw him stiffen, and she automatically glanced over at

Rand. His eyes were on Alex, and his expression had become slightly troubled.

Therefore she wasn't surprised when it was Rand who answered her. "Alex and I were both there for a time right after college," he said smoothly. "Alex and I were roommates in college. It was a great time. Our antics are still discussed with awe among undergraduates there. Right, Alex?"

"Right."

"We both donate money regularly, I think in large part due to the guilty consciences we both possess."

"Speak for yourself, Rand." Alex had begun visibly to relax at his friend's change of subject.

Montaraz was not mentioned again, and somehow Rachel couldn't find the courage to reintroduce it. As the evening progressed she found herself enjoying the constant banter between the two men. They talked of their college days and their travels, suitably censoring the more risqué parts, she was sure. It was obvious that they had a great respect and admiration for each other beside the deep underlying friendship. By the time the fruit and cheese were placed on the table, Rachel had begun to enjoy herself.

Alex lounged back in his chair and looked pointedly at his friend. "Don't you think it's time you excused yourself to the guesthouse?"

Rand sighed dramatically. "Must you be so obvious in your desire to get rid of me, Alex?"

"If you were a good guest, I wouldn't have to be so obvious."

"Oh, please," Rachel inserted, "don't leave on my account, Rand. I need to get home soon anyway."

"Are you kidding?" Rand immediately rose to his feet. "If you left, Alex would never forgive me." He strode around the table and took her hand. "Rachel, it's been my great pleasure. Somehow I think we'll be seeing a lot of each other, so for now it will only be 'good night.' " He bent and placed an elaborate kiss on the back of her hand, then turned toward the plainly exasperated Alex. "I'm going, I'm going."

Alex waited until Rand left the room, then turned to Rachel with a wry twist to his lips. "You'd never know he was a heart surgeon, would you? But he is and a damn good one too."

"That's what I understand. The surprise is that you two are such good friends." As soon as she said it, she regretted it, because all casualness left Alex and he reverted to the intense, almost harsh man she had seen the night of the storm.

"The surprise being, I suppose, that such a wonderful person as Rand could have such a terrible person as myself for a friend?"

Rachel felt herself color and knew she deserved her embarrassment. How could she have been so tactless? And it hadn't been what she had meant at all. "No, really— I just meant— It seems unusual for two such powerful but different men to be good friends."

"Never mind, Rachel. I know the rumors you've probably heard. I'm sure you can't help but wonder about them."

"Oh, not really. . . . I guess I was just curious, like everyone else. . . . But I know how people exaggerate."

"They're all true."

"I beg your pardon?"

"The rumors—everything you've ever heard

about me—they're all true. Now, shall we have coffee in the salon?" He rose and assisted her out of her chair, but Rachel was only vaguely aware of it. She was still stunned by his calm assertion that all the rumors about him were true.

They reached the salon before she found her voice. "Then you were actually a mercenary in Montaraz?"

He waved her to the forest-green velvet sofa in front of the fireplace. "If you want to call a young, idealistic man, fresh out of college, fighting for what he thought was freedom, and the democratic way, a mercenary, then yes, I was a mercenary. I was a paid soldier, fighting for a country that wasn't my own." He eyed her keenly. "Now that you know, do you want to leave?"

"No." She had wanted to leave as soon as Rand had retired to the guesthouse for the evening, but now Alex was actually revealing some of himself to her, and she discovered she wanted to stay.

He smiled at her, but the smile was uncommonly cold. "Do you find my past exciting?"

There sounded as if there were something hurtful in the hard tone of his voice, as if he were trying to hurt her. Or could it possibly be that he was the one who was hurting?

"Should I find your past exciting?"

"A lot of women do."

No, she had been mistaken, she decided. His tone was completely devoid of emotion. She turned away from him. "Actually," she said levelly, "I was thinking of the children, the babies who must have been hurt, or killed, or who lost their parents."

"Rachel?" He had said only her name, but it

was in a way that oddly warmed her. She looked back at him. "Would you like a brandy?"

"No, just coffee will be fine."

"Good, I'll join you." He gestured toward the engraved silver tray that had been set up before the couch. "Would you please pour?" He waited until she began, then asked, "Are you very upset with me for maneuvering you into coming tonight?"

"I was," she admitted. "I don't like to be maneuvered by any man. But actually I've rather enjoyed this evening. It's been interesting."

He chuckled. "That's a very candid answer, Rachel. Most women would have tried to play a game with me, perhaps put on a show of pouting about being *coerced* into coming tonight, when in reality they would have been panting to come." He shook his head and smiled. "Sometimes I don't quite know how to handle your honesty. It throws me."

She handed him his cup, wondering if she could trust the sincerity she thought she saw in his smile. She decided she couldn't. "I can't believe that much of anything throws you."

"Believe it." He paused to take a sip of the coffee. "You said you didn't like to be maneuvered by any man. Is that why you're determined to marry for money? So that you can be in control?"

"Why are you so interested in the fact that I told you I'm going to marry for money?"

"I'm curious. I've never known a woman to admit it."

"Well, you're partly right about the reason. But mostly it's so that I will never, ever have to worry about money again." She didn't understand why, but she didn't mind telling him. Maybe it had to do with the wish that, if one said something enough times, it would come true.

"Do you? Worry about money?"

"Everyone who doesn't have it does. I want to give my grandmother and my sister things they've never had before. I want to live in a big, beautiful house like this one. I want to be able to sleep until noon if I choose. I want to have breakfast in bed and be waited on by servants."

"And have jewels and pretty clothes?"

"Yes, all of it."

"And you don't think you'll have to pay a price?"

There. He had unerringly put his finger on the soft spot in her plan, and all her doubts about Sean resurfaced. She stood and paced to the center of the room, all at once deciding that she needed breathing space, away from Alex. "What's too high a price is to allow myself to love again. And if you're talking about paying a price with my body, I can bear it."

"I wasn't, but we can start there. You say you can *bear* it?"

The intense concentration he always seemed to focus on her was getting to Rachel. It was, she felt, like being in the direct line of a laser beam. "That's right. Sex was invented by men for their own exclusive pleasure."

Alex gave a great shout of laughter. "Aren't you forgetting about Eve and the apple? Surely she invented sex."

"She couldn't have known what she was doing until it was too late." How had they gotten on this subject? Rachel wondered. She had no desire to talk with Alex about sex, but now he had managed to put her on the defensive, and she couldn't let the subject go without trying to explain. "Sex is something I'll have to tolerate in order to get what I want."

"Tolerate." He shook his head slowly, and his voice took on a new edge. "Whoever he is, he really did a job on you, didn't he?"

He had done it again, she thought with agitation. He had slanted the angle of their conversation toward something she did not want to talk about. And although she knew that Alex wasn't angry at her, she suddenly felt threatened. A strange tingle began to dance down her spine, awakening nerve endings, and her scalp tightened. It was the beginning stages of panic, and she recognized the signs easily. "What?"

"Who is he, Rachel, and where can I get my hands on him?"

She thrust her fingers through her hair. "I—I had better go."

"Wait." He rose and crossed to her side, close enough so that she could see the darkness that had appeared within the depths of his eyes, a darkness that riveted, and disturbed, and held her absolutely immobile. "Who is he?" he asked softly. "I want to know."

"You've got no right to ask," she murmured weakly.

"You're right, but I'm still asking." He gently slid his hand up the side of her face until he was almost cradling it. "Rachel, you've been hurt so badly. Tell me about it. With my past and my attitudes about life, I'm not sure I'm capable of helping anyone, but strangely I want to try."

She laughed, and even to her ears she sounded on the verge of hysteria. "No one can help me but myself."

"Who is he, Rachel?"

"Why do you want to know?"

"Because I must."

She felt trapped, as if he had backed her into a corner, but when she looked around, she realized she could move—leave—anytime she wanted. He had even removed his hand from her face.

"That's no answer, Alex," she said quietly.

"That's all the answer I have right now." He laughed, a laugh directed at himself, as if he, too, couldn't understand it, and it was the laugh—so uncharacteristic of the man—that broke things free within her. One moment she was saying to herself, *I'm not going to tell him, I'm not going to relive that pain,* and the next moment she proceeded to do that very thing.

"His name was David."

"And you had an affair with him."

"Yes. I was in Atlanta, working hard to make my dreams come true, lonely and without many friends. David was an executive in the Fashion Mart. He took an interest in me, and soon we were dating. I was flattered. He was handsome and popular, and at last I felt I belonged, that my dreams were coming true. He made all sorts of promises and, fool that I was, I believed him. Fool, because he was really a first-class louse. But he never gave himself away. Not in any way. Not until I told him I was pregnant."

"Pregnant!"

"The night I told him I was pregnant he was the epitome of understanding. He would pay for the abortion, he said. He would stand by me. But when I told him I would never have an abortion, he changed. Oh, it was subtle, and it wasn't until I looked back on it, months later, that I realized it.

He still insisted that he would be there for me, probably to keep me quiet and avoid any unpleasantness. He even came around for a while. And me—I built more dreams. Of white picket fences and a pink and blue nursery.

"As soon as my stomach started to grow, however, his visits became fewer and fewer, until they stopped altogether. And then I finally had to face the fact of just how alone I was. There was no question of inflicting my problems on Gran. She's had so much to deal with in her life, I just couldn't bring myself to do it."

"Too proud?"

"Too scared. I was so scared, but, oh, how I wanted that baby."

"What happened?" Alex asked quietly.

"One night I went into labor. It was too soon, much too soon. I was all alone. There was a storm. I called an ambulance, but it was delayed by the storm." Her throat had tightened with tears, but she forced the words to come. "My baby was delivered on the way to the hospital. She could have lived. She should have lived. But there were complications, and the ambulance attendants weren't prepared. My baby died that night, in a blinding rainstorm. I never saw David again."

The silence that fell in the great room after her words was stunning. Alex felt angry . . . and helpless. He didn't understand why it should hurt him that Rachel was standing before him, all color drained out of her beautiful face, telling him this. And he didn't understand why this woman, who seemed able to reach him on so many levels, should have had to go through an experience like that.

All he knew in this moment was that it was such a waste—a waste of a precious life, a waste of beauty, a waste of innocence. Waste was something Alex had seen too much of; it was something that he deplored.

But he understood, and he silently applauded Rachel. She had had a terrible tragedy in her young life. It might have defeated her. And it would have done a lesser person in. But she had come out fighting; granted, in a way that most people would look down their noses at. But not him. He understood, because he had reacted in a very similar way to an equally devastating experience. It made him want to draw her close.

"Come here." The command was very soft.

She wanted to; that was the odd thing. She really wanted to go to him and let him take her in his arms and soothe away the hurt. But that would be out of the question, of course, and not in her plan.

"No."

"Why not?" he asked gently. "You once told me you were scared of no man. I only want to hold you, to wipe away your tears."

"There are no tears to wipe away, Alex." She lifted her face to him. "See. The tears you saw the other night at the dance were the last. There will be no more."

"You sound very determined. And you think marrying for money will solve everything."

"That's right." She gave a pathetic little laugh. "It's a genuinely terrible thing to do, but I'm tough and I'll pull it off."

"Oh, yes, Rachel," he murmured hoarsely. "You're so tough. You're so tough that all I've been able to think about doing since I met you is holding you and feeling your skin beneath my fingers." His arm curved around her before she could respond, and he led her to the velvet couch with the many pillows that sat in front of the fireplace. "But still, tonight I just want to hold you."

"No, I can't."

"Listen to me, Rachel. All of us, no matter how tough, sometimes need someone to hold on to. Hold on to me for a while."

What he said touched her deeply, but still she asked, "You?" with tears she had said were gone forever springing into her eyes. "You're too hard, Alex."

"Yes, I am, and that means I have more than enough strength for both of us. Come here."

So she did. In hours that were suspended out of time, she lay with him in front of the fire, not speaking, not thinking. For this one little bit of time, she decided to take with both hands the solace and comfort this extraordinary man was offering. She knew tomorrow would return things to their proper perspective. And tomorrow she would again think of Sean and the future she had planned out.

Five

Light poured from the windows of the house, bathing the porch and the young woman who sat there in a pale illumination. It picked up the ivory color of the loose-sleeved cotton caftan, pearlizing it and making the woman who wore it appear translucent, otherworldly.

Rachel wearily leaned her head back against the rattan porch chair, musing that if the night before had been something out of a dream, today had certainly brought her back to reality with a vengeance. It was only nine o'clock, but at the moment she couldn't summon the energy to climb the stairs to her bed. Jaime was sleeping over at a girlfriend's to study for an upcoming test, and Gran had gone to bed directly after dinner. Rachel supposed that, for her age, Gran's health was generally good. But then again, Gran seemed to tire more easily these days, and it worried her a great deal.

She cast her mind back over the day, trying to remember why she was so tired. Mr. Sifferman had been in a dark mood, not so unusual a happenstance in and of itself. But when she had received a personal phone call, his mood had positively blackened. The call had been from Alex, but Mr. Sifferman had no way of knowing it, and Rachel had had no intention of telling him. Alex had called because he wanted to see her again. She had refused. Just refusing Alex had taken a considerable amount of energy, and she wasn't sure why it should be so.

She shut her eyes. The light autumn breeze brought a pervasive smell of pine. Overhead the high-pitched drone of cicadas roosting in the pines and live oaks was almost continuous. Rachel hardly noticed any of it. If the cicadas had suddenly stopped their drone and silence had fallen over the night, then Rachel would have given heed. But these sounds, these smells, were part of her world, and tonight her mind was on someone who wasn't. Alejandro Doral—a compelling man, a dangerous man.

The dragonlike roar of an engine broke through her thoughts, and surprisingly her heart leapt, thinking it might be Alex. It wasn't. It was Sean, drunk, and angrier than she had ever seen him. He nearly fell out of the snazzy sports car he drove and began weaving his way to the porch.

"So you're here." His words were slurred with the effects of too much whiskey.

"Here I am," she remarked coolly. "Where did you think I would be?"

"With that high and mighty Alex Doral," he

sneered, advancing on to the porch. "Who else? I heard all about you having dinner with him last night. Did you think I wouldn't?"

"To tell you the truth, Sean, I really didn't give the matter any thought."

"Forgot all about me, did you?" He lunged for her, grabbing her arm. "Did you let him hold you, kiss you, make love to you? Did you let him do all the things you've never let me do?"

"Sean, let me go!" His fingers were biting cruelly into the flesh just above her elbow.

"Not until you tell me that you love me."

Her stomach turned over at the thought. "Sean, you're disgusting; you absolutely reek of liquor."

"Sure, sweetheart!" He jerked her to him threateningly. "*Now* you think so. Now, when you've got Doral on the line. But before"—his fingers dug deeper into her skin, and she bit her lip to keep from crying out—"before it was just you and me. You wanted me then. Do you remember?" Abruptly he ground his lips into hers until she could taste blood that she was sure was hers.

Rachel didn't know what to do. Of primary importance to her was that her grandmother not be awakened and upset. A hundred ideas crossed and recrossed her mind as she thought of her options. She knew if she stopped resisting Sean, he would cease hurting her. And she knew if she talked real sweet to him, she could dissolve his anger. It had worked in the past, and she knew it would work now.

But somehow this time she couldn't bring herself to do it.

Scenes from her childhood came rushing back to Rachel, and she remembered all her mother had experienced at the hands of her father and how she and Jaime had suffered as a result. And she remembered how Gran had sacrificed and given these last thirteen years to raising two girls at a time when she should have been enjoying retirement—and all because of an alcoholic . . . like Sean.

And in that moment it became crystal-clear to her. No matter what the price to marry Sean for his money, it was way too high.

She stopped fighting and went slack in Sean's arms, and as soon as she did, he loosened his grip.

Pawing at the neckline of the caftan, he whined, "Aw, honey, I don't want to fight with you, but I get so damn jealous."

"Sean, you're doing it again. You're blaming your drunkenness on me, and this time I refuse to take the blame. It's not going to work. It's over. I don't want to see you again."

He jerked her closer, ripping the neckline until it was at least two inches deeper. "Rachel! You can't mean it."

"I've never meant anything more in my life. Get out of here, Sean! You're a drunk and a louse and I can't abide either."

"Come on. You want me and you want my money."

"Your money," Rachel lashed out disparagingly. "That's a laugh. You get your money from trust funds set up for you by your family. You've never earned a dime in your life."

He gave her a sloppy, boozy grin, and she felt her skin crawl. "I know what you're doing. You're just playing with me. You want me to ask you to marry me. So all right. I'll do whatever it takes to have you. Marry me, Rachel."

It was absolutely amazing, Rachel thought. There wasn't even a flicker of a doubt in her mind. She knew now that she could never, under any circumstances, marry Sean.

"No, Sean. I'm sorry, but it's over. Please accept it and leave."

He grabbed her again at the exact same place on her arm as before, and this time she couldn't help but cry out from the pain. "You bitch!" he snarled. "You're not going to do this to me. You've teased me for weeks, and when I finally ask you to marry me, you say no. Well, I'm not buying it. One way or another you're going to be mine."

She tried to struggle, but his other hand gripped her throat and began tightening. Over his shoulder she saw the beam of a car's headlights, and when it turned into her driveway, she couldn't believe her luck.

"There's somebody here, Sean," she gasped in desperation, more to distract him than anything else.

"What?" He turned toward the oncoming lights, but didn't release her. With every second that passed, Rachel realized dimly, Sean was coming closer to cutting off her air completely.

Alejandro Doral slammed out of his car, vaulted over the picket fence, and made it to the porch in a couple of long strides. He took one look at Rachel's pale face and the cruel hold Sean had on her, then turned on Sean. "Let her go, Dillingham." Alex's voice was barely above a whisper, but it was the most menacing sound Rachel had ever heard.

Sean released her immediately, and Rachel didn't blame him. If Alex had ever spoken to her in that voice, she would probably have curled up and died.

"Leave."

One word, but—spoken by Alex in that soft, deadly way of his—it had its intended effect.

"She's not what you think, you know," Sean sneered. "She's nothing but a tease. She won't put out unless you marry her."

Under the silk shirt he was wearing, every muscle in Alex's body appeared tensed, coiled, ready for action. "Do you want to leave on your own two feet, Dillingham, or do you want to be carried away on a stretcher?"

"I'm leaving," Sean muttered sullenly. He turned an ugly face on Rachel. "When Doral leaves town, you'll want me back, and then you'll have to crawl on your hands and knees."

Rachel shuddered as cold chills swept through her body. She felt just as she would have if a snake had uncoiled itself from around her body and had slithered off.

Alex saw Dillingham's car lights disappear into the distance, then turned to Rachel. Her face was as pale as the color of her caftan, and she was looking at him with eyes that were large and frightened. It occurred to him that she might be as frightened of him as she had been of Dillingham. He knew exactly the impression his rage had made on Dillingham, and it couldn't have been lost on her either. He forced his fists to unclench. The last thing he wanted was to frighten her. Raising his fingers to the thin, sensitive skin that covered the pounding pulse in the side of her neck, he stroked it and pretended not to notice when she flinched at his touch.

"Did he hurt you?"

"No, I'm fine." Alex heard the tremor in her voice and had to fight harder than ever to get his own anger under control. She said, "Thank you for stopping though. I don't know what I would have done if you hadn't." She waved a hand vaguely toward the second story of the house. "My grandmother is sleeping."

"I'm glad I happened to be driving by." He deliberately gentled his voice. "I half intended to stop if I saw a light. But when I saw you struggling, you couldn't have kept me away."

"Sean was drunk," she murmured dully, her eyes following the route his car had taken.

"Getting rid of Dillingham was the best thing that could have happened to you."

"Maybe." She laughed weakly. "I don't know. All I know is that I had to do it."

"You could never have gone through with marrying him, no matter what you say. If it hadn't happened tonight, it would have happened soon."

"You sound very sure."

"I'm coming to know you better all the time, Rachel."

"Are you?" She tilted her head at an angle so that she could see him better in the dim light. "I'm not a very likable person, am I?"

"Don't ever say that again." He reached for her arm, just above her elbow, but immediately released her when she gave a small cry of pain. "He *did* hurt you!"

"No, I—"

"Let me see." He pushed the sleeve of the caftan up until he could see the deep bruising already beginning. "The son of a bitch," he said calmly, coldy. "I should have killed him."

"Alex!"

He glanced up and saw the alarm in her face. "Don't be frightened, Rachel. It was only a figure of speech."

She didn't believe him. She had seen the merciless rage on his face. She had seen how he held his hands. And she believed, as she had never believed anything else in her life, that he could have killed Sean with one blow of those lethal hands. The same hands that were reaching out for her now.

"Come here, Rachel." He saw what she was thinking and he didn't blame her, but he did regret it deeply.

Even though she remained standing in the shadows, her fear of Alex had lasted only an instant. She knew his background, knew what he was capable of doing. But she also remembered the way he had held her last night and somehow, in some way that she couldn't begin to explain, she knew that he wouldn't hurt her. Physically, that is.

But he was still dangerous, and she spoke her thoughts aloud before she could stop herself. "You're like a fire, Alex. It would be so easy to let you warm me. But I can't. Because if I let myself get too close, I'll be burned."

As always her honesty shocked him—and made him want her more than ever. Her caftan gaped open, revealing the top of her alluringly firm breasts. He wanted to take them into his hands, but for the moment he resisted. "Get burned, Rachel. Catch on fire with me. I promise it will hurt good." He pulled her out of the shadows until she was standing in the soft, warm pool of light with him, then he took his hands away from her. "Give yourself to me, Rachel," he whispered hoarsely. "Let the fire bring exquisite pleasure to us both."

Bending his head to her lips, he opened his mouth on hers, lightly, lingeringly. Rachel's hands were tight fists at her sides, indicative of how hard she was trying to resist this man, this man who was like no other she had ever known. The tip of his tongue slid across her mouth, tasting her, feeling like roughened velvet on her lips. She moved her head restlessly, and in the process moved even closer to the heat of his body.

He felt her involuntary response and had to fight to keep his arms from closing around her. Instead, he slipped his tongue between her lips and had the satisfaction of hearing her moan. The inside of her mouth was exciting beyond belief, and he plunged his tongue deeper.

He wasn't touching her anywhere except her mouth, yet Rachel found herself pressing against him. And when his tongue surged against hers, she gave a throaty moan once again and curled her arms around his neck.

Still he did not enclose her in his arms. He could feel the tips of her breasts, evocatively pointed, through the cloth of her caftan, and he realized she must have very little on underneath. In his mind he remembered how he had imagined the rigid imprint of her nipples against the amber chiffon of her dress the first night he had seen her. And it made him want to feel the satin nakedness of her breasts against the palms of his hands, and to taste the sweetness of her nipples with his mouth that much more.

His body transmitted his need to her without words, without touch, and Rachel found she had no resistance to the power of it. She did something she had never done before with any man. She took his hand and guided it inside the torn cloth of the caftan to her breast, then gasped at the initial shock of pleasure it gave her. There was no clumsiness or awkwardness to his touch. He took her breast into his hand as if it belonged there, running his thumb over the nipple until the heated pleasure she felt began throbbing between her legs.

"I want you, Rachel," he murmured. "Come home with me now. Let me show you what it can be like between a man and a woman."

She felt as if a fever was upon her, a delirium. He raised his head, but his hand was still caressing her breast and his eyes were burning her with a jeweled fire. She had never felt more helpless in her life. "Alejandro."

His hand stilled and tightened on her breast, and it seemed as if her heart had stopped. "What did you call me?"

"Alejandro," she whispered dazedly. "That's your name."

"Yes, Rachel, that's my name," he breathed against the scented softness of her neck. "Will you come with me to my house, let me make love to you until you forget all the cold ugliness of your past and can only remember the sweet, hot heat of our two bodies joined?"

Rachel struggled with herself to resist, but his words and his hands on her skin were fast dissolving any objectivity she might have regarding their situation. "No, Alex," she managed to gasp. "Don't ask me again."

"Why?" He didn't want to, but he raised his head away from her. He was curious about the nearly desperate note in her voice. "Will you come with me if I do?"

"No, I can't. I can't." She hated the sound of

the sob in her voice, but she couldn't seem to do anything about it.

"Is it the money?" he asked. "Because if it is, I'll give you however much you want."

She pushed away from him and clenched her teeth together. "I'll tell you what I told Sean. I will never again give myself to a man without the security of marriage. I will never again love a man."

"Security," he murmured, brushing back the hair from her face. "You're making this harder than it has to be, Rachel."

"Don't ask me again, Alex. Don't come around again. You're too strong for me. You make me forget my resolves."

"Evidently not." He gave a harsh laugh.

"Almost. You *almost* make me forget. And if we were together very much, I'm afraid I would forget. There's something about you, Alex, and I find it's very hard for me to say no to you."

His fingers on her cheek were oddly gentle in contrast to the strength of purpose she could read in his face. "Really? That's very interesting . . . and informative. You shouldn't be so honest, Rachel. You're giving me the ammunition I need—and don't think I won't use it."

"You won't have the chance, because from now on I'm going to stay far away from you."

"Will you? We'll see. We'll see."

The next days became a trial for Rachel just to get through. Alex didn't try to contact her directly, but he came to the bank every day, sometimes twice a day. She had no idea if he had a legitimate reason to be there or not, because he didn't come to her window, going instead to the ecstatic Mr.

Sifferman. Most of the time he wouldn't speak to her, only nod in her direction. A few times he would say hello, ask after her grandmother and Jaime. And always the intensity of his eyes unsettled her.

And when he wasn't there in person, people talked about him. About his plans for the mill. Would a man such as Alex Doral, who had profit-making ventures all over the world, be willing to take on a losing proposition such as the paper mill?

Everyone knew that the plant hadn't been updated since it was first built at the turn of the century. The plant took a tremendous amount of energy to run, and with the escalating cost of oil, coupled with the fact that people weren't willing to pay that much more for their paper bags and cardboard boxes . . . well, one could almost see the writing on the wall. It would surely take a staggering amount of money to redesign the plant and make it cost-effective and energy-efficient. It seemed much more likely, everyone decided, that he would just take a loss on it, thus taking advantage of a tax write-off someone in his position must surely need.

There were a lot of gloom-and-doom predictions and no one felt worse than Rachel. She knew now she would never be able to marry for money. And that left her with a problem. If the paper mill shut down, she would be forced to go to Jacksonville, and the thought of living away from Gran and Jaime was almost more than she could stand. So like everyone else she waited to see what would happen with the paper mill and watched Alejandro Doral from afar. And she and Gran made plans for Jaime's thirteenth birthday party.

* * *

One afternoon Rachel emerged from the bank utterly exhausted. A long evening stretched in front of her, one in which she needed to finish the dress she was making for Jaime. Normally she would have looked forward to it but not tonight. The work at the bank was getting her down. It seemed to her that Mr. Sifferman was singling her out more and more for criticism, and it wasn't entirely her imagination either. A few of her co-workers had come up to her behind their manager's back to commiserate.

"Rachel." She looked up to see Alex waiting at the curb, leaning against his long, low car, the door ajar. "How about a ride home?"

She crossed the sidewalk to him, feeling her heart begin to thud with the same extravagance it always did whenever she saw him. "No, thank you."

"You look tired. You're working too hard."

She frowned, annoyed that what she felt could so easily be seen by him. "Look, I'm fine, and I have a way home. The bus will be along in a few minutes."

"I insist," he said smoothly, grasping her arm and inserting her into his car. "Besides, we're drawing a crowd."

One look over his shoulder told her the truth of his statement. Her fellow employees, all getting off work at the same time, had congregated just outside the entryway to the bank, gawking at the sight of the most powerful man in town offering a ride home to one of their own. Rachel closed her mouth on her objections. In moments Alex was beside her in the car and they were on their way.

Rachel was torn between her urge to protest and the excitement of being close to him again. The urge to protest won out, though, because it affected her pride. "How could you do that to me? Do you realize the explanations I'll have to make in the morning?"

"Just tell them the truth. That I was afraid you'd turn me down if I called and asked you out, so I decided to kidnap you."

"One of these days, Alex, you're going to have to learn to take no for an answer."

"Maybe. Maybe not. At any rate, not today. I wanted to see you and here you are."

"Okay"—she crossed her arms over her chest and settled back into the leather cushion—"what do you want?"

"Not yet. Not yet."

He didn't speak again until minutes later, when he pulled the car onto a secluded bluff overlooking the river. Silently he swiveled in the seat and just studied her for a moment. "How have you been?" he asked softly.

"Fine," she answered automatically. It was the same answer she would have given him if she had been running a hundred-and-three fever.

"I gather Sean has stayed away from you."

She started in surprise. "He has, but how did you know?"

"I've kept a pretty close eye on you."

"Really?" She shifted uncomfortably. The idea that he had been watching her made her feel an odd excitement in the pit of her stomach.

"Do you want me to have Mr. Sifferman replaced?"

"What?"

"I know he's been making your life hell at work, Rachel."

"How could you possibly know that?"

"I've made it my business to know things about you. I've seen the way he looks at you and talks to you. You're young and pretty and bright. I think he sees you as a threat."

"Me? But I don't want his job!"

"But you could do it, probably better than he could. And the customers like you much better than they like him."

She stared, confounded.

"Of course, there's another alternative. You could come live with me, give up working."

"Are you out of your mind?" she asked slowly. "I would never do that. I may not be going to marry Sean now, but that doesn't mean I've changed my mind about anything else. I'll never let a man make love to me who is not my husband."

"Why not? Because the act of making love to a man is so disagreeable that you need other compensations, such as the security of a marriage?"

"That's right."

"I could teach you differently."

"You *think* you could because you have a colossal ego."

He smiled. "Do you remember the night on your porch not so long ago when you were in my arms and you called me Alejandro?"

"Yes." Too well for her own peace of mind, she thought ironically.

"That night, if I had kissed you one more time, if I had asked you one more time to come home with me, you wouldn't have been able to say no, and I could have shown you an ecstasy you've obviously never known."

"But it didn't happen," she said rather desperately. "And it won't. If you'll just stay away from me . . ."

"Why don't you ask something easy from me, Rachel?" he remarked dryly, before turning and firing up the engine of his car.

That night after dinner Rand watched Alex as he stood by the window, staring blankly out into the night. "Have you made up your mind about the mill?" Rand asked.

Alex rotated to face his friend. "I think so. It's going to be hard, but I'm going to completely redesign the plant."

"That's quite a decision."

"It'll involve millions,"Alex confirmed succinctly, "and I'll have to shut the plant down for six months to a year. But this town needs that mill to survive. Besides the people who work in it, there are elderly people who receive pensions and dividends from it."

"Why, Alex," Rand mocked, "is this actually a humanitarian decision on your part?"

"What's the matter?" He paused in the act of lighting a cheroot to give his friend an amused look. "Don't you think I'm capable of such a decision?"

"Oh, absolutely. I've just never known you to admit it, that's all."

"Well, I'm admitting it." Alex blew a steady stream of smoke out his mouth and nostrils. "Satisfied?"

"Not yet. There's another element in this decision, isn't there?"

"I'm not sure I know what you mean."

"Rachel Kirkland. I think she's the main reason you've decided to stay here and refurbish the mill."

"Let's change the subject, shall we?" Alex flung himself into his desk chair and eyed his friend seriously. "Are you still determined to go to Montaraz?"

Rand let out a long whistle. "Boy, when you change the subject, you really change the subject."

"The question stands."

"All right, then, you know I am."

"Rand, all my information indicates the country is about to go up in flames. El León's government is about to be toppled."

"So what's new? His regime hasn't been that stable for a long time now, and I've been getting in and out without too much trouble."

"This time is different, Rand. I've got a bad feeling."

"All the more reason to get my medical supplies in there before it happens. There'll be a lot of people needing my help."

"But your personal safety can't be guaranteed."

Rand laughed. "Since when has that ever stopped either of us?"

"Listen to me," Alex ground out tightly. "El León has turned a blind eye to your comings and goings because he knows you're apolitical, and somewhere in that black heart of his he knows you're helping."

Rand smiled, not the least put out by his friend's anger. "It's not because of me, my friend, it's because of *you*. El León has let me get away with my activities because of your association with him. You were with him both at the beginning and at the end, and you're one of the few people on this earth he respects."

"Then pay me back," Alex urged. "Don't go. There are a lot of people right here in the States who can benefit from your expertise. Now would be the perfect time to start that clinic we've talked about so often. You're already on a leave of absence, and funding wouldn't be any problem."

For the first time Rand's expression turned grave. "I've made a lot of promises, Alex. I won't go back on them. Like you, I've learned I can't change the world, but I can change little parts of it. In our own ways we both do it."

"Dammit, Rand. You're as stubborn as—"

"You," Rand supplied with a grin, his mood changing yet again. "*You*, my friend. And getting back to the subject you so neatly changed, namely Rachel, I think you've finally met your match."

Six

"You two are the absolute greatest!" Jaime pronounced from the backseat of Gran's old car. "This is going to be the best birthday *ever.*"

Rachel laughed, glancing at her sister in the rearview mirror. "You're going to have to calm down, honey, or you're going to disintegrate into a smoking pile of nervous energy before the party."

"Not a chance. This is my first boy-girl party, and I'm going to have a ball." She looked into her purse-size mirror once again. "I can't believe what they did to my hair!"

Rachel and Gran had picked up Jaime from the beauty shop, a special treat to go along with the new dress Rachel had made for her, and Rachel didn't know who, of the three of them, was the most excited.

"You should know by now that you have beautiful hair," Gran scolded. "Heaven knows, your sister and I have told you often enough."

"I know," Jaime breathed, staring at the glossy red ringlets atop her head with wonder, "but they actually managed to *tame* it. Can you believe it?"

"Absolutely," Rachel proclaimed. "And I hope you're going to be as pleased with the decorations I put up. They're not much—just crepe paper and balloons—but I think they're very festive."

"I bet it all looks great. Gran, I can hardly wait to see the cake you made me. You've been so secretive about it."

"A special birthday calls for a special cake. You'll see soon enough."

Jaime gave a little squeal of excitement. "I don't think I can wait."

"Well, you won't have to wait much longer," Rachel said, pulling the car into their driveway, "because here we are, and your guests will be arriving in a couple of hours."

Jaime jumped out of the car as soon as it stopped and headed for the front door. Gran followed, but Rachel was a little slower. She was so happy that she and Gran had been able to give this little party for Jaime. She knew it wasn't much by way of most teenager's standards these days, but Jaime was one of those rare individuals who had learned to be happy with very little—bless her heart, Rachel thought lovingly, she had had to—so it was important to Rachel that they had been able to do this for her.

Rachel was strolling up the walk when she saw Jaime jerk open the front door and come to a dead stop. Gran halted behind her, looked over her shoulder, and gave a loud gasp. Unable to imagine what could be wrong, Rachel raced up the steps to them.

"What's wrong? Gran? Jaime?"

Jaime bent down to slip off her shoes, then stepped forward into the house. Gran did likewise, their actions finally giving Rachel the chance to see what on earth had startled them. And when she did, she, too, halted at the door, incapable to taking one step forward.

"Oh, my God," she murmured.

The house looked like a disaster area. Water was running down the walls from the second floor, saturating the once gaily twisted and draped crepe paper. Red, white, and blue was bleeding down the walls and onto the soaked floors. Plaster from the ceiling had broken off and fallen onto the cake already positioned in a place of honor on a card table set in one corner of the room, and bits of wet plaster coated Gran's cherished furniture.

"The upstairs water pipes must have burst," Gran said dully.

At the sound of her grandmother's voice Rachel came out of her shock and took in her appearance. Her grandmother's face was ashen and her hands were trembling. Heedless of her shoes, Rachel went to her immediately and gently took her by the arm.

"Gran, I think you and Jaime should come out on the porch. You can sit there while I go shut off the water."

"No, no. There's so much to do. I must start cleaning."

"No, Gran. You need to get out of here. We don't know how much damage has been done to the ceiling. Look at it. It's bowing. It could collapse at any time."

"I need to get my pictures," Gran mumbled. "Maybe we could pull the couch out on the porch."

"Jaime, help me," Rachel called, then caught

her first glimpse of her sister. Silent tears were rolling down Jaime's young face, but when she realized Rachel needed her, she made a gallant effort to wipe them away. "Rachel's right, Gran, come on."

"There's some things I need to see about," Gran was saying in a frightening monotone. "I can't leave things as they are. There's work to be done."

"What's happened here?" a masculine voice boomed out. "Rachel, are you all right?"

Rachel jerked around, her eyes fastening on Alex as if he were the only thing left stable in a world that had suddenly begun to disintegrate.

"Alex! Help me get my grandmother out of here. I'm afraid the ceiling is going to collapse."

At once Alex came to the other side of Gran and took her other arm. "I'm Alex Doral, and I'm going to help. Let's go out on the porch and you can tell me everything that you want done." He began to guide her out the door.

"Oh, no, I can't. You see, I must go upstairs and get the necklace my husband gave me the day we married. It's very important. It's made of garnets and pearls, and it's quite beautiful."

"I'm sure it is," Alex soothed, gently refusing to let her stop when she would have. "And I promise you I will get it for you and anything else you want." He led her to one of the porch chairs and settled her into it, then turned to Rachel, his eyes taking in everything about her with lightning speed. "Are you all right?"

"I-I'm fine." She ran a distressed hand through her hair. "I'm just worried about Gran and Jaime."

Alex turned swiftly to see Jaime standing behind him. He smiled kindly, taking in her tear-stained face. "Hi. I'm Alex. Are you okay?" She nodded. "Good. Rachel? Where is the water cutoff?"

"Around back, underneath the kitchen window." She pointed more or less in the general direction. "I'll take you."

"No, you stay here. I'll be right back."

Rachel did exactly as he said, mainly because she didn't know what else to do. Her heart was breaking, seeing her grandmother—usually so proud and strong—nearly defeated, and her sister, who had looked forward so much to her first teenage party, trying to be so brave.

She went to Jaime and took her in her arms. "It's going to be okay. I promise. Somehow we'll come out of this."

"I know, I know. Don't worry about me, Rachel. You've got too much else to think about now."

Alex bounded up the stairs. "The water's turned off. I think I'd better go in and assess the damage. However, just from what little I've already seen, I don't think you'll be able to live here for a while."

Rachel spoke before she thought. "But we don't have anywhere else to go!"

"Yes, you do. My place." Before she could object, he had already disappeared into the house.

She followed him in. "We can't stay with you. It wouldn't be right. I hardly know you."

Instead of answering her directly, he asked, "Someone was having a birthday party?"

She nodded miserably. "Jaime. It was to be her thirteenth. She was so happy."

"She'll have her party," he said decisively. "At my house."

"B-but that's impossible. It's in two hours. You can't arrange a party and contact all the kids in two hours." He strode to the phone and punched out a number, leaving Rachel to follow in his wake. "Besides which, we can't stay with you. We can't impose."

"Carlos?" Alex said into the phone. "As soon as I hang up, get on the phone to town and order a birthday cake for—" He paused and looked at Rachel.

"Twenty," Jaime supplied hesitantly from the door.

Alex rewarded her with a warm smile. "Twenty. It must be ready and at the house in two hours. Then call the Yacht Club, tell them it's for me, and arrange to have some birthday decorations delivered within the hour, plus see what you can do about other refreshments. It should all be suitable for a birthday party for a thirteen-year-old girl." He smiled again at Jaime. "A very beautiful young lady named Jaime is going to have a party. Right. Also, have three guest bedrooms prepared immediately. That's right. Now get Rand on the phone for me, will you?" During the lull his eyes turned on Rachel, successfully penetrating her weak defenses with their knowledge and determination. "Do you have any other place to go?"

"No," Rachel admitted reluctantly.

"Do you think your grandmother is in any shape for us to argue about this?"

She shook her head.

"And do you want your sister to have her birthday party?"

Rachel looked at Jaime, so pretty with her freshly done hair, and thought of the dress she had spent such long hours over, hanging upstairs in her closet. Since the pipes were in between the floors, she assumed their clothes would be intact.

"Rachel, whatever you think is best is what we'll do," Jaime said quietly. "Don't worry about me. The kids will understand."

Rachel's heart turned over. For someone so young, Jaime was so valiant and unselfish. She made her decision. "Yes, I want Jaime to have her birthday party."

Alex's eyes seemed to warm, but he didn't say anything directly to her. "Rand? Listen, grab the pickup truck and drive over to Rachel's. The water pipes have burst here, and I need your help. Right. See you in a few minutes." He hung up and turned to face Rachel. "Everything is settled."

Viewing her sister, red-cheeked and laughing, dancing to the beat of the latest popular rock song, Rachel breathed a sigh of satisfaction. The party was almost over and could without a doubt be called an unqualified success. For one thing the kids were endlessly impressed with the fact that the party was being held at Alex Doral's estate. For another the party had been miraculously pulled together by Alex, Rand, and Carlos in under two hours. All Rachel and Jaime had contributed to the party had been to call Jaime's friends to tell them of the change of location.

As for Gran, Alex and Rand had managed to get everything she had asked for out of the house and had stored it at the mansion. Gran had made a brief appearance at the party, then had gone to the pretty, fresh room Alex had given her to rest. Much to Rachel's relief Alex had insisted that Gran's doctor come to give her a checkup, and Gran had given in without so much as a demur. To her amazement Rachel was finding that her usually strong grandmother was putty in Alex's hands and that Jaime was fast developing a giant-size crush on the man.

Rachel supposed she should worry about it, but she simply had too much else to worry about. Tops on her list was the question of how in the world they were going to be able to afford to repair the house.

"What do you think?" Alex asked, stepping in front of her. "Is my first effort at throwing a teenage party a success?"

Rachel laughed in spite of her worries. "Yes, and Alex, I can't thank you enough."

"A whole different subject entirely," he murmured, smiling and drawing her away from the music out onto the terrace.

She followed but laced her fingers together nervously. "Look, I don't quite know what we're going to do, but I promise we won't impose on you long. I'll think of something."

"Nonsense." He motioned toward Jaime. "Your sister is quite happy to be here. Your grandmother is being taken care of. What more could you want?"

She shrugged, reluctant to put her concerns into words to a man whom she couldn't even describe accurately as a friend. Just what he was doing in her life was something she would have to figure out later, she thought. "We have insurance," she assured him. "It's just that I don't know how much of the repair costs it will actually cover," she admitted.

"Don't worry. I think we both agree, your grandmother is the most important person to be considered here. Her happiness, her health. We'll do what we have to do to make sure that both are taken care of."

"You keep saying 'we.' I can't allow myself to become indebted to you."

"Why not?" He touched her face. "Would that be such a terrible thing?"

"I've told you before," she said, stepping away from his touch, "no man will ever have control over me." She saw the amused, almost sensuous look in his eyes and became frustrated. "And besides that, I don't know *why* you're doing this."

"Does it matter?"

"Of course, it matters. Tell me why."

"Not now," he said softly. "Just for tonight, enjoy yourself."

"Rachel, Rachel!" Jaime called. "Come dance. You and Alex come dance."

Alex's eyes twinkled down at her in the most disarming fashion. "You heard your sister. There's an old Spanish custom that every wish should be granted to a young girl on her thirteenth birthday."

Rachel glared at him, but Jaime squealed, "Really?"

He laughed and took Rachel's hand, leading her onto the dance floor. The kids had put a song with a slow, throbbing rhythm on the record player, one about love that lasted and moonlight that never dimmed. It was impossibly romantic, Rachel thought.

Alex held her so close that she could feel every hard variation of his body's muscle. Reflexively the points of her breasts tightened, and one look into Alex's eyes showed that he had felt it. She could sense a hot electricity arching from him to her, filling her with a heat that threatened to undermine all resolves. And then his desire began to grow against her, and she looked up into his eyes and started to tremble. The swiftness with which passion overtook her surprised her.

With the kids enjoying their participation in Jaime's party so much, she couldn't protest. She tried to hold herself as stiffly as possible and not look into Alex's beguiling eyes again, but it was no use.

His body moved against hers with a fluid strength. His hands splayed out across her back, pulling her into him until she ached with a profound awareness of him. Desire blazed unmistakably. He was seducing her. And later she had to admit to herself that the only thing that had stopped the seduction from happening was the song's ending and the kids' applause, bringing her back to some semblance of reality.

Living in Alex's home was an answer to a prayer. Unfortunately it was also a continuous trial to Rachel. Even before she found out that most of the furnishings and art were Alex's, Rachel had known that the house and the man somehow seemed to fit each other. He roamed it like some exotic jungle animal, though completely at ease. Constantly watching her. Waiting. And when he wasn't there, his presence remained; filling the empty spaces, surrounding her, breathing her in and out. Or so it seemed.

Gran was content for the time being, and Jaime was thriving. But Rachel's nerves were slowly shredding.

One morning about a week after they had moved in, Rachel sat at the breakfast table alone, her brow contracted with anxiety. The damage to Gran's beloved house had taken its toll on her, and she was sleeping later than usual. Jaime wasn't down either and if she didn't hurry, she'd be late for school.

Rachel stared back down at the pile of estimates she had received for repairs on the house. Her fears had been realized. Their insurance would cover only about half the cost. What was she going to do? Gran would never be happy living anywhere else.

Just then Jaime bounced in, out of breath, her hair flying. "Don't have time for breakfast. See you this evening."

"Wait a minute," Rachel protested. "You've got to eat something."

"Don't have time," Jaime repeated, downing a third of a glass of orange juice with one gulp.

"Your sister is right," Alex commented dryly from behind Rachel, evidently just coming into the room. "Sit down and eat a proper breakfast, and I'll have Carlos drive you to school."

"Gosh, no! A chauffeur and everything. Are you kidding? I'd die!"

"She's nothing like you, is she?" Alex asked Rachel quizzically, coming around the table and taking the place across from her. "Come on, Jaime. At least take a piece of toast."

"Oh, okay," she agreed cheerfully, and grabbed a handful of toast. "Bye now."

Rachel shook her head and once again lowered her gaze to the papers in front of her.

"Your sister's exuberance certainly livens up my home."

"Mmm." She glanced around the table. She supposed she should try to eat something. If only she didn't have to work today, she might be able to go over to the house and start some of the work herself. She could certainly paint. She'd have to peel off the old wallpaper first though. She hoped Gran wouldn't want new wallpaper, because she didn't have the slightest idea how to go about papering. But then again she could learn. Of course, she couldn't do any of that until the plumbing had been replaced, and she sure couldn't do that.

"Rachel?"

"Mmm?"

"I'm trying to talk to you."

She looked up with a start. "I'm sorry, Alex. What is it?"

"I was asking what has put that frown on your face. It's been there almost continuously this past week. Aren't you comfortable here?"

"Comfortable? Yes, certainly," she declared, although *comfortable* was not a word she would use to describe her feelings whenever she was around Alex.

"Rachel." His voice cut determinedly across her chaotic thoughts. "It's your grandmother's house, isn't it? What are those papers in front of you? Estimates?"

She nodded dully and ran her hand through her hair. "Our insurance is not going to begin to cover everything, and I don't know what I'm going to do."

"It won't be a problem."

She looked up. "Why?"

"I'll pay all expenses not covered by insurance."

"I can't let you do that!"

"You can't *not* let me do it. This has nothing to do with us, Rachel. It's for your grandmother."

She slumped in her chair. He was right. Gran

was everything. "I'll pay you back, every penny. It may take a while."

"I'm not asking for repayment, but I won't argue with you about it. If you feel you must, then you can pay me back a little every month. But only a little. I don't want it to be too hard on you."

"Why are you being so kind to us?"

The edges of his mouth lifted crookedly. "You think I'm being kind, Rachel? I think I'm being pragmatic. I know you well enough by now to know that Jaime and your grandmother are your primary concerns. If they are taken care of, you will have more time for me."

"No, Alex."

"No?" He looked at her for a minute. "Do you even know what you're saying no to?"

She remained silent.

"It's there between us all the time, isn't it?" he asked softly. "The fact that I want you and you want me."

"I don't want you," she denied hotly.

"Ah, Rachel. Where's the honesty now?" He paused. "There's nothing you can name that I won't give you. Try me."

"*No!*" she practically screamed. "No, no, no." Throwing her napkin on the table, she rose and made for the door, but the deep timbre of his voice stopped her.

"One of these nights, and very soon, you'll stop saying no to me, Rachel. Or maybe you'll just say no in a different way."

Seven

Thrusting the reports away, Alex shut his eyes and pinched the bridge of his nose, willing away the pain behind his eyes. Sometimes he thought that if all the business reports he had ever read were laid end to end, they would encircle the globe ten times over. And if this eyestrain kept up, he mused humorously, he would find himself needing glasses.

Opening his eyes once more, he saw that the fire in front of him was dying. He snapped off the lamp beside his chair, leaving only a small light on the desk in the corner of the room, and settled more deeply into the cushions of the glove-soft leather of the easy chair.

He supposed he should go upstairs to bed. Tomorrow would be another long day. His attention and energies would once more be divided among the problems of running a far-flung business empire from a small town in Florida and the seemingly endless decisions regarding the mill. In addition there was his worry over Rand's trip to Montaraz. He knew Rand planned to leave soon. He had used all his contacts there to try to ensure Rand's safety, but in the end he knew they would be of no use if El León was overthrown.

And then there was Rachel. Always in the center of his mind. Beautiful Rachel, living beneath his roof and doing her best to avoid him. Desirable Rachel, just doors away from his own bedroom. Rachel, the real reason he couldn't sleep.

The house was completely still. Outside a fine mist of a rain was falling. Rachel turned over in bed and looked again at the clock. Midnight. The witching hour. The end of one day, the beginning of another. Yet neither one really. Caught—a time in-between.

She smothered a groan. She was so restless. How was she ever going to be able to sleep? It had been this way for two weeks now, ever since she had moved into Alex's house. Flinging aside the covers, she slipped out of bed. Warm milk, the conventional treatment for insomnia, did not appeal to her, but the library downstairs did. Perhaps she could find a sufficiently dull book and read herself to sleep.

The terrazzo in the entry hall felt cool and smooth beneath her bare feet. She supposed she should have taken the time to put on a robe and slippers, but she had been feeling too unsettled even to think straight lately. Now, though, she noticed for the first time the discernible dampness in the air. Suddenly she shuddered and rubbed her bare arms. The thin peach-colored nylon of her gown flared out from her body as she turned into the corridor off of which the library opened. She knew no one else was awake, but nevertheless, she breathed a sigh of relief when she at last entered the library.

In the whole of this great house the library was her favorite room. Mainly because, even though it was quite large, it was one of the coziest, with the shelves of books, the rich smell of leather, the large mahogany desk, the long velvet-covered couch, and assorted chairs. A thickly padded, intricately patterned Oriental rug covered the floor, and a marble fireplace was set deep into one wall.

Rachel saw that the room was in virtual darkness, except for a lamp that illuminated a pale yellow square on the desktop, and the low fire burning in the fireplace. Alex. She could feel his presence. He must have only recently left the room. She started toward the fire.

Alex saw her—Rachel, who suddenly by some magic of his mind had been conjured up. Real, gliding past his chair and toward the fire, her slender body backlit by the fire through the thin cloth of her gown.

"Rachel."

"Oh!" She twirled, startled. "I'm sorry, I didn't see you."

The firelight highlighted his high cheekbones and called attention to the hollows that lay beneath. He sat very still, yet there seemed to be an incredible amount of motion in his stillness. Rachel could feel the heat of the fire on the back of her body and a different kind of heat the length of her front. His eyes were searing her, and she felt her pulse begin to hammer.

"I—I didn't mean to disturb you. I'll leave."

"Don't go." His words were soft, as if he didn't

want to disturb the air between them. "I can't sleep either."

Slowly he stood and took the few steps necessary to reach her, his eyes covering the pale beauty of her face and the aureole of dark hair that contained touches of the firelight within it. He wanted her. He had wanted women before, he acknowledged, but Rachel was different. Special. She was amber fire and silver tears, and he wanted her unrestrictedly.

He could sense the indecision in her eyes. "Don't go," he said again. "Please." Then before he could think to plan what he was going to do next, he cupped her face in his hands and looked deep into her eyes. "Rachel, I want you more than anything else in this world. Please want me in return."

Her breath caught in her throat at the entreaty in his voice, and unknowingly her lips parted. Alex groaned and lowered his mouth to hers, compellingly urgent and achingly tender, and the combination was like dynamite blowing her apart.

Her hands slid over his shirt and felt the heavy pounding of his heart. She had never before wanted to touch a man, but now her fingers slid inside the opening of his shirt to feel the warmth of his skin and the crispness of the hair that covered it.

His tongue thrust deeper, and she opened her mouth wider, wanting it, accepting it. Then his hand slid down her spine to her buttocks and pressed her into him until she could feel the magnitude of his desire for her. The effect of the two blatantly sexual acts made her go weak with a hot longing. Fire shadows reached out into the room, dancing over the walls and the rug and the two interlocked bodies.

Picking her up, Alex carried her to the chair. She fit perfectly in his lap, her rounded bottom cushioned over his swollen sex. He wrapped his arm around her and brought her close, resting his mouth against the soft skin behind her ear. For a minute he did nothing, content to have her near, her perfumed warmth enveloping him like a night cloud. He knew now that her fragrance was completely natural, owing nothing to artifice, and it was the most erotic scent he had ever smelled.

He felt a need to taste it. Flicking his tongue to the vulnerable point, he licked lightly. Liking the almost sweet taste, he drew a portion of the skin into his mouth and began to suck lightly.

Rachel squirmed in his arms, barely aware of the tiny moans that were emanating from her. She had never before known that such sensual sensations could streak through her body, fire her blood, and inflame her mind until coherence fled. She writhed against him and had the satisfaction of his mouth returning to hers.

Impatient now, his hands went to the tiny buttons that ran down the front of her gown and hastily undid them. He wanted to feel her silk-smooth flesh against his own. When his hand finally reached beneath the gown to grasp the firm roundness of one breast, he thought he might go over the edge, but he felt Rachel cease to breathe for a moment and tempered his response. He must remember that this woman quivering beneath his hands had never known the ecstasy of satisfaction.

He pushed aside the gown and feasted his eyes on the glowing skin. Her breast filled his hand; her nipple stood rigid and infinitely tempting. His lips traced a tautened cord down the side of her throat, pausing at the base of her neck, then continuing over the rise of her breasts until they closed on the tip.

Rachel felt the demand of his mouth instantly and the acknowledging response between her legs. She was helpless. Her body seemed to be answering him even before he asked the question. And then he did, and she had to come to terms with what was happening.

"Are you going to let me make love to you?" Alex questioned hoarsely.

So there it was again. The question that had been between them since the first night they met. She knew her answer. It was the same answer that she had so easily given to all the men who had come into her life since David. But somehow she knew that this night was different, this man was different, and she was afraid for herself. The excitement welling up within her was almost too strong, yet somehow she managed to gasp out "No."

But at almost the same time she was saying that, his hand was traveling down the curved line of her hip until he reached the folds of her nightgown. She was completely naked underneath the gown. She knew it and he knew it. Therefore, when his hand began to edge beneath the hem and slowly smooth its way up the length of her leg, she thought her skin might ignite under his touch.

"Say that again," he murmured.

She did. "No." But this time, the no was fainter, and she could feel herself beginning to weaken.

His hand slid to the inside of her thigh, where the skin was softer, more vulnerable and infinitely more sensitive.

"Say it again."

"Alex," she pleaded shakily. "No."

"Say it again, Rachel."

His hand stopped at the apex of her thighs, at the point of her body that felt the hottest, the heaviest. "Alex, I . . ."

His fingers slipped inside the womanly folds and began gently to manipulate the sensitive tissue, inflaming every nerve in her body. "This feels wonderful, doesn't it? Think how much better I could make you feel if I were inside you, full and hard. Think about it," he growled, "and say no to me again."

"I can't!" The words were torn from her as her body arched against his hand. "I can't." She tossed her head feverishly against his shoulder. "You can do it, Alex. You can take me and make love to me, and God help me, I'll probably help . . . but I'll *never* forgive you."

His fingers stilled. His chest heaved. Slowly he moved his hand until it was on top of her gown and lying limply against her waist. His head dropped back against the chair, and for a long minute there was silence while he fought to regain control.

Rachel did the same, each nerve in her body still pulsating its need for assuagement. She was totally bewildered and very much afraid, for now she knew that this man, Alejandro Doral, could make her crave him to the point that the rules she had come to live by were only a thread away from being broken. If he hadn't stopped, he could have commanded anything of her, and she wouldn't have fought him. She couldn't have.

Finally Alex drew in a deep breath and raised his head. "Oh, Rachel." His voice was husky, and he absently reached for a strand of her hair to stroke. "I wish you had said anything but that. I think I could have ignored anything but that."

"I don't understand."

"I'm not sure I do either. But I think it's time that you went back upstairs."

Rachel flushed with embarrassment. She had totally forgotten that she was still curled up in his arms. She slipped off his lap. Wrapping her arms around her waist, she looked at Alex, uncertain of what to do next. She was reluctant to leave things as they were between them. For some strange reason she felt she should apologize.

He raised one foot and placed it on the ottoman. "What is it, Rachel?" he questioned sardonically. "Have you changed your mind?"

She could feel his eyes burning through the semidarkness to her, enwrapping her with the desire that still smoldered between them, and she laced her fingers together nervously. "I feel I should explain, but I'm not sure what to say. It's just that you make me feel things that I'm not sure how to handle."

"Ah, Rachel," he sighed wearily. "We're a pair, you and I. I want you and you want me. Yet because of something that happened in the past, you won't let me make love to you. You won't forget about the past and live with me in the present a day at a time."

"No," she agreed quietly, "because I'll be the one who pays in the end. Just like with David. He wasn't the one whose screams filled the night when he was told our baby was dead. I was."

"Rachel," he said, his tones low and measured, "I'm sorrier than I can say that you had to go through that, and I could kill the man who caused you to. It's because of him that you can't forgive *any* man."

"That's not true," she denied hotly, then stopped. Oh, no, it was true! She hadn't realized it before, but she had been trying to make every man who said he wanted her pay for what David had done. She supposed it was just one more thing to mark against herself. "Alex, y-you've been very kind to me, to my family, and I certainly don't hate you."

He smiled at her, and there was a knowledge in the curve of his lips that troubled her. "But you would if I laid you on the floor in front of that fire and showed you that pasts can be forgotten."

An image flashed into her mind of the two of them lying entwined in front of the fireplace. It was a troubling, exciting image, and she couldn't get it out of her mind.

When she didn't answer, Alex prodded, "Wouldn't you, Rachel?"

She pushed a shaky hand through her hair. "I . . . I think I'd better go to bed."

Alex reached for a cheroot, pausing to light it before he spoke again. "I think you'd better."

The rest of the night was hell for Rachel. It seemed to stretch to eternity. Thoughts of Alex's lovemaking churned through her mind and pulsed through her body. And one question kept coming back to her: Had she been telling the truth when she said she wouldn't have forgiven him if he had made love to her?

The rain stopped about three, and she finally fell into a troubled sleep about four. When Carlos knocked on her door at seven with a tray of coffee, Rachel was awake.

The coffee was welcome, but Carlos's message was not. It seemed Alex wanted to see her in the library as soon as possible. She hurriedly downed the coffee and dressed in a pair of tailored beige slacks and a rust-colored blouse. Mr. Sifferman frowned on his women employees wearing slacks to work, but it was the best she could do this morning.

The first thing she noticed when she entered the library was that the fireplace was cold and empty. The second thing she noticed was Alex. He was standing behind the desk, his black hair highlighted by the morning sunlight that was streaming through the open windows. He wore dark blue jeans, pressed, creased, and fitted to perfection, and a cream-colored V-neck sweater that showed a mat of crisp black hair through the opening. An intricately braided chain lay around his neck, gleaming very gold against his brown skin. He looked masculine and formidable and . . . tired. Evidently he hadn't gotten much sleep either.

"Carlos said you wanted to see me before I went to work," she said uncertainly.

"Sit down, Rachel."

"I—I don't have much time, Alex."

Silently he pointed toward a wing chair in front of the desk. She sat down and waited, trying to ignore his steady regard that was playing such havoc with her nerves. She was very much afraid of what was coming. She was certain he was going to ask them to leave his house, and she couldn't really say that she blamed him.

He walked slowly around the desk and perched on the corner, one foot on the floor, one foot slightly off, causing the material of his pants to stretch tautly over his muscled thighs.

Although she wasn't eager for him to ask her to leave, his continued silence was so unnerving, she found herself speaking. "Why did you want to see me, Alex?"

"There's something I want to ask you."

"Yes?"

He looked down at the toe of his boot for a moment. "Will you marry me, Rachel?"

"M-marry you?" she repeated.

There was a quiet humor in his voice. "You say that as if you've never thought of it before."

"I haven't!"

He flexed his foot and allowed a small ironic grin to touch his mouth. "The thing of it is, I believe you. You wanted to marry for money, but I don't believe I ever once crossed your mind as a possible candidate for a husband. I can think of at least a few women who would question your logic."

She jumped to her feet, unconsciously wringing her hands. "But you're totally unsuitable!"

One black eyebrow shot up. "Really? What makes me more unsuitable than Sean Dillingham? I can promise you I'll never get so drunk that you'll have to ride home with someone else. And I'll never abuse you physically." He caught her arm as she paced past him and brought her to stand in front of him. Because he was still sitting, their faces were level and close. She could smell the musky scent of his freshly shaved skin.

His nearness confused her, and before she could think she blurted out, "I don't love you, Alex!"

His blue eyes were glittering, but his expression was inscrutable. "I know you're not interested in love, and as I recall, I don't think I've ever asked you to love me either."

As he had done so many times before, he once again left her speechless. He was asking her to join him in a marriage where there would be no love, something she had said she wanted. So how could she refuse him when he was offering her exactly what she wanted? Yet her every instinct told her to do that very thing.

"If you're going to spend your good money for a wife, Alex, don't you think you ought to buy one who at least loves you?" she asked.

"Let me worry about whether or not I'm getting a bargain," he said insistently, then gave a small laugh. "The trouble with you, Rachel, is that you underestimate yourself. When you look at yourself, you see someone who was defiled by a man and who now has grown so hard that she is determined to marry for money. When I look at you, I see someone who is honest and courageous, and who has great love for her family. Believe it or not, those qualities are all too rare, and they are to be valued highly."

He had a way with words, Rachel thought fretfully. And he also had a way with his voice and his hands and his lips. Excitement coiled through her as she admitted to herself that Alex Doral affected her deeply and traumatically, and *that* was the reason she could never marry him. She would never be the one in control. She tried to pull away, but he wouldn't let her.

"Rachel, stop and think about this for a minute. I'm offering you everything you've ever told me you wanted."

"It won't work, Alex," she protested.

"Why not? Is it that you don't believe I'll give you the things I say? I will, you know."

"Things?" she questioned, confused. She wasn't sure what he was talking about. All she could think about was the heat from his body, which seemed to be permeating hers.

His voice softened. "Listen to me, Rachel. Let me take care of you."

"Take care of me?"

"I want to be in a position to protect you from men like David and Sean. I want to take care of Jaime and your grandmother for you so that you'll never have to worry about them. I want to give you the security you've never had. Believe me, Rachel."

There was never a question that she didn't believe him. In a way she wished there were. It would make it so much easier. But he was being honest with her; on that one thing she was certain. For all the exotic glamour that seemed to surround him, she had learned that he lived his life on a very basic level. Whether it was a trait he picked up because of his past, she didn't know. But he had no time for playacting or dissembling. It was why he admired her honesty so much.

"I don't understand you, Alex. Last night—"

"Yes," he murmured, running his hand up her arm, caressing her arms through the soft material of her blouse. "And there's definitely that." His voice turned husky with desire. "I no longer ache with wanting you, Rachel. The ache has turned into a pain, a pain so severe that it's as if I'm being clawed from the inside out." He drew her closer, so that the breath from his words heated her lips. "Marry me, Rachel. Take away my pain and let me take away yours."

She moaned. Alex was the most complicated

man she had ever known. He was a self-professed mercenary, and a shark of a businessman who held the fate of a whole town in the palm of his hands. He was a man who could seduce a woman as easily and as casually as he could choose an entrée for dinner. Such a man could never become her husband.

Then why was a part of her remembering all his kindnesses over the past few weeks to her and her family? If only he hadn't said he wanted to protect her and to take care of Jaime and Gran. If only he weren't so achingly gentle when he held her in his arms. Like now.

His mouth touched hers and moved slowly back and forth. Opening his legs wider, he pulled her closer so that the pleasure centers of their bodies were touching, throbbing. She shuddered at the sudden heavy sweetness that coursed through her. Her arms went around his neck and she moved sinuously against his hardness.

His mouth was tasting hers, his hands were slowly inflaming her. "Say you'll marry me, Rachel. I promise you, you'll never be sorry."

"All right."

Her assent surprised her as much as it did him. He pulled away from her and brushed her hair away from her face. "Yes?" he questioned.

She nodded, caught up in a cloud of desire.

He drew in a deep breath, then slowly exhaled it. "Good. I'll contact my lawyer. He can be here by this afternoon. We'll draw up a premarital contract that you can be happy with."

"What?" Premarital contract? What was he talking about?

"Don't worry." He smiled softly as he readjusted her blouse. "He may be my lawyer, but the contract will be infinitely fair. You won't have anything to complain about."

"Alex, I—"

"I want you to give your notice today. No, on second thought I'll do it. You won't even have to go back there. Knowing Sifferman, he'll give you trouble.

"No, wait! If anyone is going to give notice, it will be me. I'm not going to leave them short a teller. I've got to at least give them time to train someone else."

He sighed, obviously not happy with her decision. "Okay. But if he gives you any problem, just walk out. Promise me you'll do that. I'll take care of him."

She shook her head. "It's happening already. You're already taking over my life."

He smiled a completely charming smile. "Isn't that what marriage is all about?"

"Marriage is an opening up of oneself to another. A bonding. I'm not sure you can do that."

"Can you?"

That stumped her. What was she doing? Here was a man any woman would give most anything to have, much less marry, and he had asked her to marry him. He said he was going to give her everything she had ever wanted. The only problem she had now was trying to decide what exactly it was that she wanted.

Things went from bad to worse. Mr. Sifferman was outraged when he learned she was submitting her resignation and predicted all sorts of doom on Rachel's head because of her "flighty" ways. She knew that if she told him that she was leaving to marry Alex, things would go easier for her, but she couldn't bring herself to do it just yet. Maybe because saying it aloud would give the situation more reality and she wasn't sure she could handle any more reality for the moment.

Trying to concentrate on her bank duties was practically a lost cause. Her thoughts kept returning to Alex. Had she really said she would marry him? She must have, she thought wonderingly, because she wouldn't have submitted her resignation otherwise. But why had she consented?

The day wore on, and she knew she was making many mistakes, but surprisingly Mr. Sifferman didn't jump on her. Instead he patted her on the shoulder, smiling, and said that mistakes could happen to anyone and didn't she want to take a break. That was when it dawned on her that Alex must have called the manager and had a few choice words with him.

That night Carlos picked her up in the limousine and whisked her back to the Spanish mansion. "Mr. Doral is closeted with his attorney, Miss Kirkland. He said to tell you that he would see you at dinner." Carlos bowed and left her standing at the front door.

"Carlos," she called after him.

"Yes?"

"Do you happen to know where my grandmother is?"

"I believe she's in the sunroom."

"Thank you."

The sunroom was at the back of the house. Wide windows allowed a perfect view of the river, and it was here where she found her grandmother taking afternoon tea. Ever since Rachel had been able to reassure her grandmother that her house would be completely restored, the older woman had relaxed appreciably. The color had returned to her skin, and Rachel acknowledged that Gran was being well looked after in Alex's home. Once a day Gran would walk over to the house and check on the workmen's progress. Alex had insisted on hiring a double crew, so the repairs were progressing very fast. The remainder of the day, she was able to rest and do nothing more strenuous than needlework. And the results were beginning to show. She was looking better all the time.

"Gran, I have something I need to talk with you about."

"Come in, Rachel. Did you have a good day at work?"

Rachel sat down beside her grandmother on the brightly upholstered sofa. "Yes . . . it was fine. Where's Jaime?"

"She's studying at a friend's house, but she'll be home in time for dinner. Rachel, what's wrong? You seem distracted."

"Gran, I don't quite know how to tell you this." Running a nervous tongue over her bottom lip, she looked worriedly at her grandmother. She didn't want the news to upset her. "I—uh—well, it seems that Alex and I are going to be married."

"How wonderful!" Gran exclaimed. "Oh, Rachel, I'm so happy for you."

"You are?"

"I've seen how the two of you look at each other. It would take a blind man to miss it. I can't tell you how relieved I am."

"Relieved?" She was glad her grandmother wasn't upset by the news, but she was a little astonished by the extent of her enthusiasm.

"Rachel, it's no secret how I've worried about you. Ever since you came home from Atlanta, you've not been yourself. But then Alex came on the scene, and you began to change. I could see it, and I hoped—"

"I began to change when Alex . . . ?"

"I don't know how to explain it, except to say you seem softer whenever you're around him."

"Softer? Do I?" That was a surprise, Rachel thought. If anything, she had tried to be harder whenever he was around.

"And of course, I couldn't ask for anyone nicer for you. Look how he's taken us in. He's been so good to us all."

That was true, Rachel reflected. Right from the start he had set out to make sure that Gran and Jaime had everything they needed. He had shown her grandmother kindness and respect, and he had given Jaime the understanding and the support that a thirteen-year-old girl displaced from her home would need, spending a lot of evenings with her in long conversations.

"Well, it seems tonight we have something to celebrate," Gran said gaily. "We must make it very festive. Excuse me, darling. I think I'll speak with Carlos."

"Of course."

Rachel absently twisted a strand of her hair and looked out at the river. It would seem that events were out of her hands.

Dinner had been a very relaxed, enjoyable affair. The candlelight had glinted off the silver, the ruby wine had gleamed in the heirloom crystal. And they had two guests—Rand Bennett and

Alex's attorney, Robert Chatsworth. He seemed to be a likeable, easygoing man, but Rachel had no illusions. He was Alex's attorney, so he was razor-sharp.

Alex, Rand, and Robert were in a jovial mood, and Gran was practically glowing. Jaime, of course, was over the moon, and Rachel continued to feel as if everything were happening to someone else, so unreal did it all seem.

As soon as dinner was over and all the toasts had been made, Alex turned to Gran. "Robert, Rand, and I have a little business to take care of. And if you don't mind, I'm going to steal Rachel away too."

"Of course not, Alex. With all the excitement I think I'll retire early tonight."

"Gran, are you feeling all right?" Rachel asked.

"Yes, darling. Just a little tired. I'll see you in the morning. Jaime?"

"Yeah, I guess I'd better go upstairs and study a little more too," Jaime grumbled good-naturedly. "That science test tomorrow is going to be hard."

Rachel had no idea what Alex had in mind, but she allowed him to usher her into the study. They were followed by Rand and Robert.

"Rachel, if you will just sit there," Alex directed, pointing to the chair she had sat in earlier that morning, "I'll show you the document Robert has drawn up for us. I think you'll find everything in order. Rand is here to witness it. Once that's out of the way, we'll set the wedding date."

"What document are you talking about, Alex?"

"Our premarital agreement," he said, handing a legal-size set of papers to her. "As I said, even though Robert is my attorney, I think you'll agree with everything in it. If not, just strike out or add, depending. With your initials beside it, it will still be considered legal."

Rachel quickly scanned the papers, and she could hardly believe what she was reading. Alex was right. It was fair—more than fair. In effect it said that if Alex decided he wanted a divorce, she would get a settlement of one million dollars. If, on the other hand, she asked for a divorce, she would get a quarter of a million dollars for every year they had been married after five years.

Her stomach churned sickeningly. To see a marriage—her marriage—reduced to numbers on a legal document made her want to cry. Which didn't make a lot of sense. But as the print blurred in front of her eyes she realized something about herself. In spite of her resolve to marry for money, a deeply buried part of her must have held on to some long-ago romantic dream regarding marriage.

"Rachel, are you all right?" The question came from Alex.

"Yes, why wouldn't I be?"

Blinking her eyes clear, she read on. Upon their marriage her debt to Alex for the repairs to her grandmother's house would automatically be dissolved. And if Alex were to die, she would get everything—the estate, his fortune, his controlling interests in businesses around the world. Everything. She dropped the document into her lap, momentarily forgetting the three men in the room. She felt as if she were suffocating. This was all too much. It was happening too fast.

Yet how could she complain? He was giving her everything she had ever asked for and more.

But, damm it, he was *controlling* her, and somehow she had to find a way to gain the upper hand.

"Rachel?"

This time it was Rand.

"Yes, I was just thinking. Could I have a pen, please?"

Her hand hovered over the paper before she started to write. She had to find a way to keep a part of herself from him or she would never be able to stay whole and in one piece.

"May I ask what you are adding?" Alex asked.

Rachel placed the period at the end of the sentence she had just written and, without looking up at Alex, started another. "I'm putting in a stipulation that says I will not be forced into having children. I will be a brood mare for no man."

There was complete silence in the room. It seemed for a moment as if the three men had stopped breathing.

A muscle jerked in Alex's jaw, before he finally said, "Fine." Then drawing a scratch pad toward him, he scrawled something on it.

She glanced up. "What are you doing?"

"I've made a note to make you an appointment in town tomorrow with the doctor."

"Why? I'm not ill."

"Birth-control pills," he said succinctly.

"Oh." She could feel herself flushing as embarrassment washed through her. She hadn't been thinking about the need for birth-control devices, just another sign that she was not thinking straight. She bent her head to the document so that her hair would shield her face. It wasn't that she didn't want a baby. She could only imagine the joy that would come from holding her own baby in her arms. It was just that she had been trying to protect herself from possible pain with the stipulation. A baby would give this man one more thing to control her with.

"Are you adding something else, Rachel?"

"Yes," she murmured, just finishing up. "We will have separate bedrooms." She initialed the two additions to the document and then handed it back to Alex. It was then that she noticed how dark Alex's face had become.

"I think not," he said, taking a pen and crossing through the last line she had written.

"Why?" she exclaimed. She knew that she would have to allow him to make love to her. After all, they would be man and wife. But she felt she needed something between them, even if it were only space, and separate bedrooms might give her the extra edge she would need to keep a distance between the two of them.

"We will sleep in the same room," he stated firmly and decisively.

She heard Rand make some sort of sound. Or maybe he had just shifted his position by the fireplace. But whatever it was, it drew Rachel's attention to him, and what she saw puzzled her. He was looking at Alex with the strangest expression on his face—as if Alex had just totally shocked him by saying that they would share a bedroom.

She looked back at Alex to see a hard, implacable expression on his face. All at once she lost the will to fight him. Why bother? she told herself.

"Okay. Where do I sign?"

Robert bent forward. "Here and here and . . . here." He indicated lines on all three copies.

She quickly signed the papers, feeling as if she were being pushed down a dark corridor without the benefit of knowing what was awaiting her at the end or whether she would survive.

"Now Rand." Robert motioned Rand over so that he could sign on the witness line. That done, Robert tucked the documents into his briefcase. "It was a pleasure meeting you, Rachel. I'm sorry, but I'll have to leave now if I'm to make my plane back to New York tonight. I'll return for the wedding, of course. By the way, Alex. When will that be?"

"In two weeks."

"Two weeks!" Rachel practically came up out of her seat.

"Didn't I tell you?" Alex asked. "I believe in short engagements. Come on, Robert. I'll walk you to the car."

Eight

Rachel remained where she was, incapable of moving. She felt as if she had just been trampled by a velvet steam roller. It was only when Rand spoke that she remembered he was still in the room.

"It's really going to be all right, you know."

She looked up and saw him smiling down at her. Between her and Rand there was no tension, no complexity. For the first time since this morning, when Alex had asked her to marry him, she consciously drew in a deep relaxing breath. "You're a nice man, Rand. I've enjoyed getting to know you these last few weeks. But in this instance I'm not sure you know what you're talking about."

He smiled and dropped into the chair behind the desk, nonchalantly swinging his feet onto the polished surface. "I've enjoyed getting to know you too. And it's reassured me."

"About what?"

"You and Alex are right for each other."

Rand couldn't have said anything that would have surprised her more. Her mouth practically fell open. "How can you say that?"

"Easily. You and Alex need each other."

"Alex doesn't need anyone," she said flatly, firmly convinced. "And anything he needs he can buy."

"Why do you say that?"

"He's the hardest, coldest man I've ever known."

The expression on his face grew serious. "It's because of what he's gone through, Rachel. Can't you understand that?"

"I guess so, but I'm not sure what that type of experience does to someone, Rand. How can a person live with the scars it must create?"

"Just like you have, Rachel." He brought his feet off the desk and sat forward. "The scars heal over and are replaced by needs that maybe only another scarred person can fill."

"I don't know, Rand. I wish he were more like you. Maybe it would work if he were more sensitive and caring about people."

"And you think Alex doesn't care?" he asked softly, almost chidingly.

Immediately Rachel felt contrite. "I admit he's been very good to my family and me. But I can never get it out of my head that he was a mercenary."

"Has he told you anything about the time he spent in Montaraz?"

"Not really. Just that he was young and idealistic."

"It's true. Remember, I was there with him for a time."

She jumped on the last part of his sentence. "For a time. Then you left before he did?"

Rand looked at her, measuring his words carefully. "Listen to me, Rachel. You need to understand this. In certain ways Alex is more sensitive than I am."

"How can you say that? You left. He stayed."

"Yes, but you see, the reason I left was because I had learned from Alex. Alex's soul couldn't take the horrors he was seeing. He burned out, went dead inside. All of a sudden I realized that the same thing was beginning to happen to me, and it gave me an advantage that I took. I left."

"And went to medical school."

"Yes, that's the way I chose to help the world. But Alex stayed on and paid dearly."

"What do you mean?" She was having a hard time understanding what Rand was trying to tell her, mainly because he was presenting her with an entirely different picture of Alex than the one she had come to know. But he was also giving her valuable clues into the deeply complex man she had agreed to marry, so she listened intently.

"In the beginning Alex was impatient to make the world a better place and he thought the sacrifices he made and saw other people making would be worth it. But in the end, El León—the man he had fought for—began showing signs of being as bad as the man Alex had fought so hard to depose. So he left and took another path in life. He decided that money was the real power in the world."

"And he set out to make a lot of it."

"Right. And he has. He's one of those people who can just look at money and it multiplies. He's also become something of an expert on Third World countries. He's respected as well as feared, and our government has called on him more than once to help ease a hot situation."

She shook her head in amazement. "I didn't know any of this."

"He wouldn't tell you. But I want you to always remember something. His scars go deep, just as yours do. You and Alex aren't so different. You're two disillusioned people who happen to have different types of scars. Rachel, just give Alex a chance. And give yourself a chance. You can help each other. You can heal each other."

The smoke from his cheroot floated upward, creating designs that soon became indistinguishable in the night, and Alex contemplated his surroundings and considered how he felt about them. He had never had a home, not really. While he was growing up his parents had lived in first one diplomatic post and then another. When he got older, he was sent away to school. As an adult, it seemed as if he had traveled constantly, staying in one place only long enough to buy, sell, start up an enterprise, or end one. Of course, he had apartments here and there around the globe, but they had never been home to him, only places of expediency.

Now he was to be married, and he knew without even asking her that Rachel would want to stay in Cypress Cove. Confronted by the thought of a real home at last, he was strangely comforted. The odd thing was that most of the things he had collected from around the world that meant anything to him were already here. His aunt had enthusiastically kept them for him. Without being aware of it, he supposed he had been making a nest in this place for a long time, and now that he had realized it, he decided he couldn't be happier.

Just then he heard a faint noise. He crouched and wheeled.

Rand held up his hands laughingly. "Take it easy. It's just me."

Alex grimaced. "Sorry. Reflex, you know."

"I know. I've just left your bride-to-be."

"How is she?"

"Skittish. Definitely skittish."

Alex looked out over the grounds. "It's liable to get worse before it gets better."

Rand smiled knowingly. "You're going to rush her to the altar before she has a chance to back out, aren't you?"

Alex nodded, taking a deep draw on his cheroot.

"You gave me something of a surprise in there," Rand commented casually.

"Oh? I didn't think there was anything I could do that would surprise you after all this time."

"I didn't either, but this definitely did. I thought you'd jump at Rachel's stipulation of separate bedrooms. There've been a lot of women over the years, Alex. And not one of them has ever had the privilege of falling asleep in your bed."

"Rachel's going to be my wife. She'll sleep beside me."

Rand's eyebrows rose. "But it's not as simple as that. What about the nightmares? They're the reason you've never wanted anyone sleeping with you."

"They're better, more manageable," Alex replied tightly.

"So you're willing to take the chance that she might see you with your guard completely down?" A grin curved Rand's mouth upward. "That's interesting, very interesting."

"They only come now when I'm disturbed or upset about something," Alex snapped dismissively.

"And I suppose you figure with Rachel beside you you'll have nothing to be upset about?"

"Exactly."

Rand paused. "You're in love with her, aren't you?"

Alex turned slowly toward his friend, showing no surprise. "Yes, I am. Totally. I didn't realize what was happening to me for a long time. All I knew was that she was the most fascinating woman I had ever known, and I had to have her. When she continued turning me down, I finally realized I must be falling in love. But it didn't come together for me until last night. I was awake all night, and when morning came, I knew for sure I was in love with her and would ask her to marry me."

Rand's face took on an expression of bemusement. "Knowing you as well as I do, I have to say this is amazing."

"That's not the word for it," Alex said wryly. "The whole idea scared me to death. But . . ."

"But?"

"But *Rachel*. The protective shell she's constructed around herself is paper-thin. I can get through it, and I know inside of her there's a lot of softness and sweetness just waiting for me. I've not had a lot of that in my life, and I want it. I need it."

"There's also a lot of hurt in her."

"I know," Alex agreed.

"In both of you."

He uttered a short laugh. "You think I hurt inside?"

"You still have the nightmares, don't you?"

Alex remained silent for a minute. "Yes, but I have a feeling that Rachel will have the power to banish the nightmares, and I do love her so. No other woman has ever affected me so strongly."

"You know, I can't quite believe that my friend—Alex Doral—is actually saying these things, but I'm glad. You deserve happiness."

"Thank you. Will you be my best man?"

Rand grinned good-naturedly. "Ah-ha! Now I know what you're up to. This is all a plot, right? You're just trying to keep me from going to Montaraz."

Alex burst out laughing. "Would that I could. No, I just want my best friend to be with me on the day that I marry. Come on, Rand. It'll be only two more weeks."

"Okay. But," Rand warned, "I'm leaving right after the wedding. Newlyweds deserve privacy."

There was a thoughtful silence, then Alex murmured quietly, "She's marrying me for my money, you know."

"Is she? Maybe. At any rate it doesn't matter. I have a feeling that the two of you will be just fine."

Two weeks was not a lot of time, Rachel soon discovered. It passed more quickly than she could ever have imagined. At first she insisted on working out her notice at the bank. But after a couple of days Mr. Sifferman informed her that they had found a replacement and her services would no longer be required, although, he hastened to add, her services had certainly been appreciated. Rachel resignedly accepted that Alex was in some way responsible, just as he was in control of everything and everyone around him.

Gran's house was an example of this. Alex had increased the number of men involved in the restoration so that Gran would be able to move back in the day before the wedding. Alex and Gran had talked the matter over and had come to the conclusion that Jaime would continue to live with Gran for a couple of months following the wedding to give the newlyweds a "honeymoon period." But after that time had passed, Jaime would live permanently with Alex and Rachel. In this way Gran would have more leisure time and still be able to see her granddaughters every day, as they would be living so close to one another. Everyone was extremely pleased with the decision. Everyone except Rachel, that is, and privately she admitted that her displeasure was only because they hadn't bothered to consult her.

Alex did consult her on other matters though. She had requested a small, private wedding, and he granted her wish. The ceremony was to take place in the church she had attended all her life. The guests were to be limited to family and friends—just under a hundred. The reception was another matter, however, and again, Alex made the decision. It was to be held at the Yacht Club, and somehow he convinced her that there were certain people who had to be invited. In the end the guest list came to around six hundred.

When the matter of her wedding dress came up, Rachel suggested a simple gown, perhaps in some pastel shade, because she felt white would be inappropriate. But Alex disagreed vehemently and insisted that the design of her wedding dress be left to him. As was becoming the pattern in their relationship, Rachel gave in, simply because he seemed to know exactly what he was doing, and she had long since lost any faith in her own judgment.

Consequently, when the day of her wedding dawned bright and clear, the dress her grand-mother helped her into was both simply designed and elaborately elegant. And when Rachel finally stood before the full-length mirror to get her first glimpse of herself, she couldn't help but let out a gasp at the radiant beauty she saw in the mirror.

The gown was made of heavy silk. And it was pure white. Alex had been very insistent about that. Its sweetheart neckline looked delicate above her breasts; the bodice was snug around her rib cage and tapered to the narrow waist, where tiny tucks flowed out into yards and yards of silk and a sweeping cathedral train. The sleeves puffed at the shoulders, then fitted down to her wrist. Reem-broidered Lyon's lace covered the bodice and a matching band edged the hem. And across the bodice and around the border of the hem dia-monds were scattered. Sparkling, precious dia-monds. A veritable fortune in diamonds.

The veil added to the absolute fantasy of the gown. A cloud of bridal illusion, it covered her head and billowed out twelve feet behind her. Rachel turned her head, and diamond-encrusted lace medallions picked up the light, glistening along the entire length of the veil.

The truly extraordinary young woman Rachel saw in the mirror seemed completely unreal to her. Her hair had been swept up under the veil into an elaborately coiled French pleat, leaving her neck bare, and to Rachel's mind, quite vulnerable. Despite the lovely autumn day outside the bedroom window, she felt ice-cold, and she shuddered.

"Wow! Rachel, you look awesome!"

"What?" Without turning, Rachel refocused her eyes on Jaime, who had just burst into the room.

"Totally awesome!" Jaime repeated reverently.

"Well, thanks. You don't look so bad yourself." Rachel twisted to get a better look at the sea-green silk organza confection Alex had chosen for Jaime. The material sprayed out to the young girl's ankles in beribboned tiers. It was quite lovely, but a frown crossed Rachel's face as she viewed the dress. The neckline was a ruffle that was currently resting low on her young sister's shoulders. Too low.

"Jaime, I think you're showing a little too much with that neckline. Why don't you pull it up a bit?"

"Oh, come on, Rachel," Jaime protested. "I don't have that much to show. Besides, I think it looks totally—"

"Awesome?" Rachel guessed.

"Rachel's right, child," Gran interjected.

Jaime swished to the mirror and twirled happily. "This is my very first long dress. And how do you like my hair?"

Rachel cast an amused expression at Gran. Jaime was making an obvious attempt to change her sister's point of attention, but neither Gran nor she were fooled.

"Alex said he wanted me to wear my hair down. He says he likes it like this! Alex says it's charming."

Somehow Rachel wasn't ready to hear about what Alex had said or what Alex wanted. "Jaime

. . ." she began, but a knock on the door forestalled her objection to her sister's neckline.

Jaime raced to the door and flung it open. "Alex!" she cried happily.

Rachel's pulse began to race as Alex walked into the room. His single-breasted tuxedo was made of a fine wool; it was so dark a midnight-blue, in a certain light it appeared almost black. The color deepened the aquamarine of his eyes, and his golden-brown skin showed darker against the pleated white shirt he wore with the tuxedo. The scar above his eyebrows and the sharp angles of his face were in contrast to the formality of his clothes and appeared at once harshly discordant and completely natural. Looking at him Rachel thought she had never seen anyone look more barbaric. And, on top of that, she thought with something close to despair, he could excite her simply by walking into a room.

"Look at my dress," Jaime was saying. "Isn't it great?" She made a pirouette, then sank into a low curtsy.

"You shouldn't be here, Alex," Gran exclaimed. "It's bad luck for the groom to see the bride before the wedding."

He smiled reassuringly at the older woman. "I don't believe in luck, Gran. I believe in making my own." After closing the door behind him, he advanced into the room. He took a long look at Rachel, then turned to Jaime. "Very, very pretty. Just as I knew you would be."

Jaime blushed. "Oh, Alex."

"And I have something here for you that will set off your new frock quite nicely."

"You have something for *me*?" Jaime squealed excitedly.

"Absolutely," Alex affirmed, taking a jeweler's box out of his pocket and opening it so that she could see the contents.

Jaime's voice dropped to a whisper of awe. "A string of pearls!"

Alex fastened the graduated pearls around the young girl's neck, then, quite casually, pulled the ruffled neckline of the sea-foam dress up over Jaime's shoulders. "There'll be plenty of time in the years ahead for you to break the hearts of the young men." Jaime's face fell, but surprisingly she didn't protest. Alex's voice held a great deal of fondness. "Why don't you run down to the salon? I believe the bouquets have arrived."

Instantly Jaime's face changed to animated excitement. "Wow! I can hardly wait to see them." She ran to the door, stopping only long enough to throw over her shoulder to her grandmother and sister, "I'll see you guys down there in a minute."

"That was very nice of you, Alex," Gran said, "but totally unnecessary."

"Nonsense." He took another box out of his pocket and approached the older woman. "Indulge me. After all, a man only marries once in his life."

The smile he turned on Rachel was one of a man who loves the woman he is about to marry, and Rachel felt an inexplicable sadness. She knew the smile had been purely for Gran's benefit. She had kept the knowledge of their marriage contract from her grandmother and sister, and she had asked Alex to do the same. It had paid off because now Gran's face was glowing at the sight of Alex's smile to her much-loved granddaughter.

Alex held out the small black velvet box to Gran somewhat ruefully. "I think you had better pin it on. I'm afraid I'd only tear the lace of your dress."

"Alex!" Gran's hand trembled as she reached for the exquisite antique brooch of pearls and garnets. "This is the most beautiful pin I have ever seen, and it will match the necklace my husband gave me. You shouldn't have." With the utmost care she attached it to her porcelain-blue lace dress. When it was finally adjusted to her satisfaction, she gave it a final, loving pat and said briskly, "Well, now I'll just leave you two alone for a few minutes. But"—she held up a warning finger— "only for a few minutes. And thank you again, Alex."

"We're family, Gran."

She put her hands on his shoulders and he bent down so that she could bestow a kiss on his cheek. "You're a very kind man."

Then with a click of the door she was gone, and Alex turned to face Rachel, a mocking expression on his face. "Do you think I'm a kind man?"

Taking off her veil, she unconsciously brought the headpiece around in front of her so that the veil wrapped around her in a shimmering white haze. She nodded in answer to his question. "You've been very kind to my family."

"But not to you?" He began walking toward her.

It was strange, she thought as she considered his question. She had the presence of mind to know that he was kind to Jaime and Gran, but when it came to Alex and her, she totally lost her objectivity. Aloud she said, "I think I'm afraid of you."

"Oh, no, Rachel. Not you." Reaching out for her, his fingers curled around the back of her neck. "Remember? You once told me you weren't afraid of me or any man."

"That was before I got to know you."

"You don't know me at all, Rachel, but you will. You will." He leaned down to cover her lips with his, briefly, tenderly. "And by the way you are the most beautiful woman I have ever seen in my life."

"Th-thank you." She fingered the veil. "Alex, this is all too much. The dress alone would have been spectacular, but the diamonds."

"The very first time I saw you, you had tears in your eyes. I said then that instead of tears you should be wearing diamonds. Well, I'm replacing your tears with diamonds."

He snapped open yet another case, only this one was larger than the other two, square and luxurious in its own right. Rachel saw the contents, and she inhaled in disbelief. In front of her on a bed of black velvet lay a collar of diamonds.

Before she had time to react further, Alex picked up the glistening necklace and fastened it around her neck. Automatically Rachel sought the mirror. The diamonds were almost knitted onto a web of platinum and gold that was so intricately fine, it resembled the lace of her wedding gown. The collar molded perfectly to the gentle slope of her throat, fanning out at the base into scallops that stopped just beyond her collarbone. Never in her wildest imaginings could she have imagined such a fantastic piece of jewelry.

Her eyes came back to the man who would soon be her husband, and she saw that his eyes had grown almost opaque, obscuring any emotion. Yet he had chosen a bridal ensemble fit for a princess. Would she ever know him as he had said? Perhaps an even better question to ask would be *Did she want to?*

"You're overwhelming me, Alex. I don't think I'm going to be able to make it down the aisle."

He lifted her chin with his finger. "Focus on me. I'll be there, waiting for you."

Nine

Rachel and Jaime climbed the steps of the church, holding great bunches of Rachel's gown in their hands to prevent it from touching the concrete. The baroque sounds of Vivaldi being played by a string ensemble drifted out to Rachel from the church. Looking up, she saw Rand waiting to greet her.

He assisted her into the vestibule, careful of her wide skirt that whispered around her. Once inside they smoothed the dress down around her. Then stepping back, Rand studied her with a broad smile on his face. "My friend Alex is one lucky man. I have a good notion to stay here and fight him for you." In spite of the humor in his voice he spoke quietly, aware of the people waiting inside the sanctuary.

Thankful to him for trying to lighten a few moments in what he was sure to know was an otherwise tense ordeal for her, she teased, "You're really terrible, flirting with a woman about to be married, do you know that? And besides that I don't believe a word of it. Wild horses couldn't keep you from your mission of mercy, much less a mere woman."

"Ah, but that's just it. You're not a *mere* woman, Rachel."

She shook her head, discounting what he said as pure flattery.

"Be still, Rachel," Jaime pleaded, fussing around the bridal gown, straightening the train and veil, taking her duties as Rachel's sole attendant very seriously.

"Did Gran make it here okay?" Rachel asked Rand.

"She's already seated, as are all the guests. It's five o'clock and the stage is set, my lovely. All we need is the bride."

Rachel took a deep, steadying breath, willing away the hard pressure she felt over her heart. "I guess I'm as ready as I'll ever be."

"Good. I'll go join Alex. Jaime, as soon as you hear the 'Wedding March' begin, you start down the aisle." He squeezed Rachel's arm and said solemnly, "Just remember, this is going to hurt me more than it's going to hurt you."

Bursting out giggling, Jaime clapped a hand over her mouth, and Rachel couldn't help but smile. "I'm going to miss you, Rand."

He dropped a quick kiss on her lips. "I'll get my kiss now, because, if I know Alex, he won't let any of us near you after the ceremony. See you in a few minutes," he said, and left.

"It's time to put your veil down," Jaime prompted.

Rachel reached for the single layer of bridal illusion that would cover her face and brought it down. The veil threw everything into soft focus.

"I hope I don't disgrace you, Rachel," Jaime whispered. "You're so beautiful. I just know I'll probably trip and fall or something."

"You're going to be just fine, honey," Rachel murmured reassuringly, accepting the elegant bouquet of five calla lilies she was to carry in the crook of her arm. "Don't you worry about a thing. I'm just so glad that you're going to be there beside me. I'm very proud of you."

"I love you, Rachel."

"I love you, too, honey."

Then the first notes of the "Wedding March" sounded, and Jaime glanced nervously at Rachel. "Okay?"

No, she thought, she wasn't okay. She had never been less okay in her life. She was about to marry a man whom she had known only a matter of weeks, and she really didn't have the slightest idea why. But she nodded and followed Jaime to the wide doors that opened onto the center aisle.

Candlelight softly lit the interior of the church, and garlands of snow-white orchids with gold satin streamers banked the altar. Alex had had the church transformed into a bower of gold and white.

Watching Jaime's halting steps down the aisle, a wild thought darted through Rachel's mind. She could still run. She could just tear off the diamond-strewn veil and run away. But then it was too late. Jaime reached the altar, the "Wedding March" swelled, and everyone rose and turned expectantly to her.

Rachel swallowed hard, acutely aware of the

pressure in her chest that was actually hurting now. Strangers and friends filled the church. Gran and Jaime. But suddenly Rachel saw only one person. Alex. Standing so straight and tall, he was waiting for her. She couldn't see his eyes, but she could feel his strong personality, pulling her to him, and she went. Step by step she drew closer to Alex, her train and veil forming a twinkling white trail behind her. Never once did she take her eyes from him, because she knew if she did, she would fall.

Unaware of the hushed gasps of admiration and awe from the congregation, she continued gliding toward Alex until she reached his side. He held out his hand, and she took it, because she could do nothing else.

The music stopped, and the minister began. "Dearly beloved, we are gathered here today . . ."

Surrounded by golden candlelight and sweetly scented flowers, Rachel felt herself sway. Alex's hand tightened firmly on hers, and his eyes glowed warmly, reassuring her, sustaining her.

"Repeat after me. . . . I, Rachel Marie, take thee, Alejandro Avarado, to be my wedded husband. . . ."

She might have been dreaming, Rachel thought, *so detached was she from what was happening around her. Only Alex's hand on hers anchored her to reality.* Her voice was barely above a whisper as she said the words. "I, Rachel Marie, take thee, Alejandro Avarado, to be my wedded husband. . . ."

"To have and to hold from this day forward, for better for worse . . ."

So much had happened to her in these last weeks, she reflected. *She had set out to marry for money, decided she couldn't, tried to ignore a man who had more money than she could even comprehend, and finally agreed to enter into a marriage with him without love.* "To have and to hold from this day forward, for better for worse . . ." she recited.

". . . for richer for poorer, in sickness and in health," the minister's voice droned in her head.

Dutifully she repeated, ". . . for richer for poorer, in sickness and in health . . ."

". . . to love and to cherish, till death us do part."

And why had she agreed? The question came back to her again, this time with a thundering force. It must be . . . No, that couldn't be! But it had to be, she thought with wonder, *because she . . . loved him. She loved him!* Her hand tightened convulsively in his and utter shock registered on her face. She saw Alex's dark brows draw together, reflecting puzzlement and concern.

". . . to love . . ." the minister prompted softly.

Faltering, she repeated, "T-to love and to cherish, till death us do part."

". . . according to God's holy ordinance and thereto I plight thee my troth."

The thing that had unconsciously been a terrible burden on her ever since she had agreed to marry Alex suddenly slipped away from her, and as it did so did the painful pressure in her chest. She wasn't giving herself to a man because of his money, Rachel realized joyfully. *She was giving herself to him because she loved him.* Her voice became stronger. ". . . according to God's holy ordinance and thereto I plight thee my troth."

The minister turned to Alex. "Repeat after

me. . . . I, Alejandro Avarado, take thee, Rachel
Marie, to be my wedded wife. . . ."

"I, Alejandro Avarado, take thee, Rachel Marie,
to be my wedded wife. . . ."

Alex's deep voice pierced her euphoric cloud.
But he didn't love her. He only wanted her. Her
heart sank.

"To have and to hold from this day forward, for
better for worse . . ."

"To have and to hold from this day forward, for
better for worse . . ." Alex pronounced the words
clearly and surely.

*She had loved David and he had hurt her.
But that love was nothing compared with what
she had come to feel for Alex. It made her all the
more vulnerable, more open to hurt, and she had
vowed never again to let a man hurt her.*

". . . for richer for poorer, in sickness and in
health . . ."

". . . for richer for poorer, in sickness and in
health . . ."

Chancing a look at Alex, she saw his eyes were
fixed on hers. She tried to see if she could find
some vestige of love for her there. But all she could
see was the reflection of candlelight in his eyes, a
flame of gold dancing in a pool of jewel-blue.

". . . to love and to cherish till death us do
part . . ."

". . . to love and to cherish till death us do
part . . ."

No, he didn't love her. But, she mused, *the
future was not as dim as it seemed. Alex had told
her that he wanted to take care of Jaime and
Gran for her. He had told her he wanted to give
her security and to protect her. Therefore,* she reasoned, *he must feel something for her. He had*

also told her he admired her honesty. She paused
to consider this last. *His admiration of her honesty was now terribly ironic, because she knew
absolutely that she was too much of a coward
ever to tell him of her love for him.*

". . . according to God's holy ordinance and
thereto I plight thee my troth . . ."

". . . according to God's holy ordinance and
thereto I plight thee my troth . . ."

"May I have the ring, please?" Rachel saw
Rand hand the minister a simple band of gold—
just what she had requested—and heard the minister begin the blessing of the ring.

How long had she loved Alex? Rachel asked
herself. *Falling in love with him must have been
such a gradual process that she hadn't even realized what was happening. She had been dead
inside for so long; but his caring, his kindness,
his passion, had seeped into her, softening her
heart until she was actually able to admit to herself that she loved him.*

She felt something warm being slipped onto
her finger and looked down to see the gold ring.

"I now pronounce you man and wife. Those
whom God has joined together let no man put
asunder. You may kiss the bride."

Alex slowly lifted the veil and carefully
arranged it around her head so that it appeared as
if a mist of diamonds had settled around her head
in a pale nimbus. Then drawing her to him, his
hand slid up the side of her jaw until his fingers
were curved around her neck, and his lips touched
hers with a pressure that held outright posses-
siveness.

Was it over? Rachel wondered. *Or was it just
beginning?*

*   *   *

The Yacht Club had never seen anything like it. There were fountains of champagne and waterfalls of rare flowers. The lavish buffet contained delicacies from around the world, and the guest list, which included friends of the bridegroom, read like Who's Who. Yachts and private planes had been arriving for the last several days, and hotels as far away as Jacksonville were full.

Everything seemed to glitter, Rachel thought wearily, even her dress and veil. There had been the reception line, the cake cutting, and the toasts, all faithfully recorded by a high-society photographer whom Alex had hired especially for the occasion. Feeling Alex's arm around her waist, she shifted her weight from one satin-shod foot to the other and let her gaze wander over the people. Somewhere in the crowd were Alex's mother and father. She had met them for the first time the night before and had liked them. They had seemed very nice and genuinely fond of their son, if a little in awe of him. She didn't blame them. Her wonder of him had grown steadily since their first meeting, and now that she knew she was in love with him, she was more in awe of him than ever.

"Tired?" Alex's voice was pitched for her hearing alone.

"A little," she admitted, looking up into the face of her bridegroom. Even now it was hard for her to realize that she was actually married to him.

"We'll slip out in a minute. Right now, though, I would like to dance with you."

"Dance?"

"The first time I ever saw you, you were

dancing—here on this very dance floor—with practically every man in the place except me."

"But I didn't even know you were here," she protested.

"I know." His face hardened somewhat. "But tonight you will."

He nodded at the orchestra leader, then led her out onto the empty dance floor. Much to Rachel's surprise the orchestra struck up the strains of "The Anniversary Waltz." What an utterly romantic and traditional thing for him to do, Rachel thought as she picked up the end of her train and veil and draped it over one arm. She had a lot to learn about her new husband, she mused, easily following his graceful lead around the floor. And she intended to do just that.

As if in a dream they danced around and around, with Alex smiling down at her and her dress floating out above the polished surface of the floor, as though the gown were made of nothing but air and sparkling lights. It was an exhilarating feeling, like dancing across the brilliant heavens and at the same time being held securely to earth. People gathered around the dance floor, remarkably quiet, but as the dance ended, applause sounded from all around them. Rachel suddenly put her hand up to her head.

"What's wrong?"

"Nothing. I just feel a little lightheaded."

Alex caught Rand's attention and had a few quiet words with him and then they were preparing to leave. The throwing of rice and the throwing of the garter were the only traditions not carried out. Rachel decided that it must be because people felt inhibited about throwing rice at a groom as commanding as Alex and a bride who was gowned in white silk and diamonds. She knew she didn't want her garter removed with all the guests looking on and had asked Alex to omit that traditional event. But she did toss her bouquet, straight to an ecstatic Jaime.

They were met at the door of Alex's Spanish mansion by a beaming Carlos and one of the household maids whose name was Ancia.

"Ancia will help you upstairs, Señora Doral, and assist you off with your gown."

A moment before, getting out of her bridal gown was uppermost in her mind. But now all that Rachel could think of was that divesting herself of her bridal raiments would be the first step toward an intimacy with Alex she wasn't ready for.

Alex saw the uncertain look on her face and asked, "Would you rather wait awhile and perhaps eat something?"

"That sounds good. I don't think I've eaten much today," she admitted. "That's probably why I got so lightheaded during our dance."

Alex lifted the veil off her head and handed it to Ancia. "Carlos, is the cold buffet I requested ready?"

"Yes, Señor. In the library."

"Fine, we'll help ourselves. Tell the staff everyone has the night off. Rachel?" He held his hand out to her.

Maybe food *would* help, she thought feverishly. At the very least it would buy her some more time. Time to get used to the newness of being Mrs. Alex Doral and, more important, her love of him.

Entering the library, Rachel saw that a fire was blazing brightly in the fireplace and white candles were flickering in tall brass candleholders. A hunt table standing behind the sofa held an elegant and enticing buffet. The familiarity and inherent comfort of the room began to soothe some of the apprehension from her.

Rachel eased herself onto the couch, trying to be as careful of her dress as she could. She really should change, she thought guiltily, but at the same time glanced back at the buffet and decided it looked awfully good.

Besides two silver buckets of iced champagne there were gleaming trays of smoked pheasant and an assortment of cheeses and frosted grapes. Black caviar, which had been mixed with grated hard-boiled egg yolk and piped into tiny eggs, tempted her from a bed of red caviar. In another dish freshly washed strawberries were arrayed around two small crystal bowls. She stuck her finger into one bowl and found it filled with whipped cream that had been mixed with sour cream. The other bowl she could see was filled with brown sugar. Using the leaves of one plump red strawberry as a stem, she dipped it into the cream mixture, then into the brown sugar. Normally the sweet and sour taste would have been a delight, but unfortunately she found herself too tense to enjoy it, and she gave up on the idea of eating for the moment.

Reaching up to her head, she began pulling the binding hairpins out of her hair. Then combing her fingers through her hair, she stripped any remaining pins and lightly massaged her scalp until her hair fell in deep swirling chestnut waves about her shoulders.

Alex had quietly joined her on the couch. "Can I fill a plate for you?"

"No, thank you. Maybe later." Unable to meet

his probing stare, Rachel looked away, into the fire. She felt such a mass of conflicting emotions. She loved Alex and she wanted him, but she also remembered that David's version of sex had been quick and thoughtless. She didn't want it to be like that with Alex. She had once told Alex she would tolerate sex with the man she married, but now she wanted so much more. She wanted it to be perfect. Being physically satisfied in lovemaking was a whole new concept to her, but she wasn't afraid of not being pleased. Knowing that Alex's experience far exceeded her own, Rachel feared that she wouldn't please him.

And there was another fear as well. During their lovemaking, when Alex had finally and at last stripped her bare, down to her deepest emotions, she had to wonder if she would be able to keep her secret of her love for him.

Alex's heart went out to Rachel. She appeared so fragile and young, with the skirt of her wedding gown flowing out around her. He knew only too well just how much she had gone through in the last couple of weeks. To his way of thinking he had pushed and prodded and ordered her around almost without mercy. And what's more, he was sure he had handled the situation all wrong. Almost daily a sense of apprehension—something quite alien to him—had invaded his normally logical and intelligent mind. He hadn't been afraid that she would run from him because he had known that her love for Gran and Jaime would keep her in his home. But the fear that she would suddenly change her mind had been so great, he had rushed her through the last couple of weeks with what must have seemed to her a terrible unfeelingness on his part.

Then today had finally come, and she was standing before him in her bridal gown. Never had there been a bride so beautiful, of that he was sure. He could have sent her the necklace by one of the maids this morning, but he had had to see her for himself. And when he had, he hadn't been sure he would be able to control his feelings. So he had gone to Jaime first, then Gran, giving himself time to become used to Rachel. He had chosen the gown and selected the diamonds himself, yet he hadn't been prepared for the complete and utter radiance of her beauty on this the day of their wedding.

Now she was his, in the eyes of God and state. He hadn't wanted anyone to have the remotest doubt about it. *Especially Rachel.* But, he reminded himself, he still had to proceed cautiously. He knew she must be nervous, not to mention tired. He saw her touch her throat, as if she had just remembered the diamond collar.

She unfastened the gems from around her neck and handed him the necklace. "You'd better put this somewhere safe."

Without even looking at it, he took it and casually lay it on the hunt table so that it rested in a glittering pile beside the caviar. "Your feet must hurt," he commented.

"What?"

Stretching down, he slipped off the white satin shoes before she had time to stop him. Then he picked up her feet and put them in his lap and began to rub. "I know how new shoes can be," he commented easily. He was rubbing the ball of one of her feet with his thumb, and once she got over the shock of his action, Rachel discovered that it felt too good to protest. "Even when they're your exact size," Alex was saying, "they still don't feel comfortable until they've been broken in." As he moved to each new area of her foot Rachel found herself reacting to the delightfully tingling sensations he was causing.

He switched to her other foot, and Rachel finally roused herself. "You don't have to do that."

"I know I don't, but I want to." He slipped out of his own shoes and grinned. "I sympathize. Standing in that receiving line wasn't a thing I'd like to repeat too often. It reminded me of too many diplomatic functions that I was dragged to as a child."

"I liked your mother and father," she ventured.

"Thank you. I like them too. It's just that we've always seen things in different ways and have never quite managed a meeting of minds."

"I don't think it's necessary for a child and his parent to agree on everything. As long as there's love and respect for one another, that should be enough."

"Maybe." He shrugged with a very Latin gesture. "But I will want to be closer to my children than my parents were to me."

Rachel felt herself growing pale. Children. She had told him that she would not be forced into having children, and he had instantly agreed. He had personally made her an appointment with the doctor and had seen that she went. Yet here he was, speaking of children as if they were very much in his plans. It could mean only that he didn't want children by her and was already looking toward the time when he would find another woman he wanted more than her, a woman who wouldn't mind having his children.

"Rachel, you've tensed up again. Turn around and let me rub your shoulders."

"No." She didn't want him to touch her—not now, not after his comment about children. "The dress . . . I might harm it."

"Don't worry about the dress." He shifted her around so that her back was to him, and she felt him release the zipper. Then his strong fingers were rubbing the tightness out of the muscles in her shoulders. Firmly, insidiously, gently, his fingers worked their magic, and his voice softened. "I'm sorry it's all been such a strain on you, but its over now and we can both relax."

"Yes," she agreed somewhat breathlessly, because slowly he had worked his hands lower, kneading the flesh on either side of her spine. Her lips parted in a silent moan. A stream of heat was traveling down her spine, keeping pace with his hands.

"Is this better?" he asked huskily.

She nodded, afraid to speak, afraid that her voice would tremble and give away the building need inside her.

"Your skin is hot," he murmured, and touched his lips to her neck. His long, lean fingers inched around her ribcage until they reached under her breasts. Briefly they brushed against the underside of one, and Rachel heard him inhale sharply. "You're not wearing a bra."

"I was afraid the line would show under the material of the dress."

"If I had known that, I'm not sure I would have made it through the ceremony so well."

She twisted so that she could see his face. "It would have affected you that much?"

"It would have affected me that much," he agreed, and closed his hands over her breasts. "I'm that hungry for you." His hands moved in circles over the sensitive skin, lifting, stroking, driving Rachel to a point where his previous mention of children was far, far in the back of her mind. When his fingers closed over the firm tips, she arched her back against him.

"Alex!"

Almost convulsively he released one of her breasts to turn her to him so that his mouth could find hers. And the kiss was so bruisingly sweet, it was agony. And it was ecstasy.

"You're mine." Alex whispered the heated words into her mouth. "You're mine!" He straightened his legs out along the sofa cushions and pulled her up against him. "Aren't you?"

"Yes, Alex," she agreed feverishly, knowing that at this point she would agree with anything he said.

"Then unbutton my shirt," he pleaded. "I have to feel you against me."

She tried, but her hands were shaking too badly and the jeweled studs in his shirt proved to be barriers she couldn't seem to overcome. He laughed huskily. "I'll do it."

"Our clothes are going to be ruined," she said shakily, realizing that her bejeweled skirt had twisted up around her thighs and the bodice had been pushed down to her waist. "Maybe we should go upstairs and change."

"We should," he agreed gruffly, peeling off his shirt and tossing it across the room. "The first time we make love together should be in a wide bed, where I can do all the things I've lain awake nights planning to do to you." He reached again for her and began working her gown off her body. "But I can't seem to stop what I've started." Once he had her gown off, he pulled her high up his chest so that he could take one throbbing pink bud into his mouth.

Rachel moaned. She had never felt like this before—excited and hot and wanting even more. Her lace petticoats stroked against her legs as she wiggled them off, letting her garter belt, panties, and silk hose follow them.

"For God's sake, Rachel. Be still." She could feel his chest rising and falling heavily. "Let me go at my own pace," he pleaded, "or I'll never be able to make it as good for you as I want."

"Yes, you will." She smiled into his eyes.

"Oh, Rachel," he groaned, and buried his face in her neck. "If you only knew."

"What?"

"How beautiful you are naked. And how hungry I am for you. Will I ever be able to get enough of you, I wonder? I want to show you so much. I want to teach you so much."

"Then teach me." She stroked his jaw and kissed him. "I'm ready. This will be my first time." *My first time to make love*, she added silently to herself, because that was what she was doing for the first time in her life.

He swept her up in his arms. "I'll take you upstairs," he said with a notable tremor in his voice.

"Will you?" she asked, nibbling on his ear.

Even though he knew there would be no servants to bother them, Alex wrapped his tuxedo jacket around her in an exceedingly protective gesture. Carrying her in his arms, he made his way out of the study and up the stairs.

Holding fast to him, Rachel marveled at the strength that allowed him to carry her so easily. New excitement coursed through her as it occurred to her what his strength would mean to her during their lovemaking. "Alejandro," she breathed into his ear.

"Rachel," he murmured raggedly, lowering her onto the step above him, so that she was standing almost level with him. "Once I'm inside of you, making love to you, I may never stop."

"Show me," she murmured daringly.

"God! How can I wait?" His mouth came down to hers with such fierceness, Rachel could only hold on to him. His tongue seemed as if it were plundering her mouth, his hands felt as if they were ravaging her body.

"Please, Alex, I want you."

"Yes," he said huskily, dropping to a carpeted step and bringing her with him, "and I want you." She gasped as she felt his hand between her thighs, finding and opening her to his searching, burning touch. Then she began to whimper.

"I know, my darling," he crooned. "I know." His teeth grated against one distended nipple, then his tongue licked away the ecstasy of hurt.

He was half sitting, half lying on the step below her, cradling her against his arm so that she was lying sideways on the step above and in no discomfort. And even if she had been, she thought feverishly, she didn't know whether she would have noticed. His fingers continued their expert probing, seeming to take her easily to some high, mysterious brink, then soothe her back from it, and then in the very next moment repeat the process all over again. Rachel's hips were undulating wildly against him.

Then suddenly with a muttered oath he lifted her and carried her the remaining distance into his room. There, with a thrilling haste, he unfastened his trousers and stepped out of them. With his eyes fixed hotly on hers he drew off the rest of his clothing until he, too, was naked. Then grasping her arms, he crushed his mouth to hers and began walking her backward the few steps necessary until she fell onto the soft bed.

Rachel had time only to take in that someone must have turned down the bedcovers before she was lost to Alex's demands. She parted her legs and felt his hardness nudging against her. She writhed, wanting him as badly as the next breath she would take.

She felt hot and cold, hard and soft, helpless and strong. It seemed as if his hands and mouth were everywhere, but in reality it was only the effects of them that she was feeling in every cell of her body. "Alex," she moaned, "I'm going to die if you don't make love to me."

"With the pleasure I'm going to bring you," he whispered as he raised his hips to enter her, "you *will* think you have died."

And then there was no more talking, only elemental sounds from both of them as he entered her. Wrapping her legs around his back, Rachel arched again and again, meeting Alex's thrusts with twists she hadn't realized she had known how to make. She was on fire and going up in flames. Just as he had said, she thought she would die.

Rachel awoke. The room had been darkened, and covers had been pulled up over her. She stirred and felt Alex's arms tighten around her.

"Alex, we've got to go back downstairs."

"Now?" His voice was deeper and more relaxed

than she had ever heard it. It made her want to curve closer into him.

"Our clothes are down there—my gown, your tuxedo, all those underthings. I'm afraid one of the maids will find it all in the morning."

Against the tender skin behind her ear—a place she was beginning to recognize as one of his favorites—he murmured, "That's what a maid is for. To pick up after us."

"But they'll know . . ."

"What?" he growled, abandoning her ear for the base of her neck. "That I couldn't wait to undress my wife and make love to her? What's so terrible about that?"

"Nothing, I suppose," she replied, loving the sensations he was creating with his mouth, but nevertheless still troubled. "But I can't stand the idea of that beautiful dress crumpled on the floor. And, *Alex*, the necklace! We just left it lying on the table."

"The idea didn't seem to bother you so much just a few hours ago." His mouth was now circling the tender flesh of one breast.

Arching her back against the sheets, she moaned, "Alex! Again?"

He chuckled. "I do have a lot to teach you, don't I? But it can wait. I just thought of something else that's downstairs that we need."

"What?" she asked, sorry now that he had stopped.

"Champagne and all sorts of food. I didn't eat much today either."

"I'll need to go to my room and get my robe," Rachel said. Raising up on one elbow, she glanced around the room for the first time. She knew that it was in actuality a suite of rooms that included the large bedroom they were in, a bathroom, and a sitting room. She had never seen any of the rooms until just now.

"All of your clothes have been moved into your own closet, which opens into the hallway of the bathroom."

"Oh?" This was the first she had heard of it, but she grinned. "Well, I didn't have many things. They couldn't take up much room."

"When I selected your wedding gown, I chose a few other things. . . ."

"A few other things?"

"Just until we had time to go shopping."

"Oh."

He got up and shrugged into a lounging robe of heavy cream silk embroidered with an Oriental design. He looked magnificent, Rachel thought, and darkly foreign.

The closet that he had designated as hers was larger than her bedroom at Gran's house. And that she had shared with Jaime. As she had told him, her limited wardrobe took up a mere fraction of the space. Across the room, or rather closet, hung Alex's "few" selections, which proved to be clothing for every occasion, from bed to an evening out. Blindly she reached for a golden negligee ensemble in shiny silk Charmeuse. It slid over her head and down her body as if it had been waiting lovingly to encase her.

Suddenly she felt terribly disoriented and bewildered. In the space of one day she had been married, wearing a dress of diamonds, to a man most sane people would run from, discovered she loved him, come back to his mansion and been made love to as she had never before dreamed possible. Could she handle all of this? She had to, she told herself firmly. She was going to make this marriage work. Without looking in the mirror, she went to meet Alex.

When they entered the library, it was to discover that the champagne had been re-iced and a fresh assortment of food had been laid out. Their clothing had been whisked away somewhere, presumably to be hung up. Even the diamond necklace had disappeared.

"Carlos," Alex murmured. "He's a good man."

"But the necklace!"

"He knows the combination to the safe. I trust him implicitly."

Rachel made her way around the sofa, wondering if she would ever become used to unseen servants doing the things she had been used to doing for herself all her life. Carlos had even managed to keep the fire going. She held out her hands to it, grateful in spite of herself. She wasn't cold, but she knew now that every time she saw a fire in this room, it would remind her of her wedding night.

A loud popping sound made her jump, and she looked around just in time to see Alex pouring a bubbling, golden liquid into tulip-shaped glasses.

"Here you are," he said, handing her one.

"What type of champagne is this, Alex? I don't think I've ever seen that type of label on a wine bottle before."

"That's not surprising. It's most rare and very expensive. So expensive and rare, in fact, it's virtually priceless. It's the private label of a world-renowned family who have been in the wine-making business for centuries. Henri Armand, the current head of the family, is a good friend of mine, and he gave me a case of it a few years back."

Rachel absorbed this in silence. This was just another indication that she was out of her element. She knew that the wines that were produced from the Armand vineyards were annually auctioned off at fantastic prices.

However, Alex gave her no time to brood. He came toward her, holding his own glass. Touching it to hers, he said softly, "To my wife," then took a sip.

"It's delicious," Rachel murmured after sampling the wine, then grimaced. What an enormous understatement, she thought. But she couldn't help but feel shy.

Remarkably Alex grinned. "It is wonderful, but I have yet to taste anything that equals the taste of you."

"Alex!" She could feel herself beginning to blush.

"Come here." He reached for her hand and drew her to the couch with him. He set aside his glass and settled her in his arms.

Rachel leaned her head back against his shoulder, at this moment completely happy. All thoughts of her insecurities were forgotten.

Smoothing his hand across the silky material that covered her midriff, Alex said, "You look enchanting in this negligee. Your body does things to the shape of the gown that I only imagined when I saw it. I like the feel of it under my hand." His hand had moved to a breast, letting the material caress her as he did.

Warmth began to flood her veins. "It feels incredible on."

Alex took her robe from her and tossed it onto

the floor. Then shifting until he was lying full-length on the couch, he drew her over him. Without bidding, Rachel opened her mouth and covered his, while her body absorbed the jolt that went through her.

"If I could reproduce the flavor of your lips, I could rule the world," Alex muttered, biting her lower lip.

"Would you want to?" Rachel asked raggedly. "Rule the world?"

"When I have you in my arms, I do rule the world."

"Alejandro," she sighed, feeling as if she were melting.

"I love the way you say my name." One of his hands had slipped beneath the low back of her gown and around to the side of a breast. The other hand had grasped the material over one firmly rounded buttock and was kneading. "Say it often," he ordered softly, "and just in that tone of voice."

"Alejandro," she whispered again.

He took her tongue into the warm cavern of his mouth, and he began to use his own tongue to lightly tease and play with it until her hips were helplessly undulating against his pelvis. His robe had worked open, and she could feel his full arousal.

"I can't tell you the sensations I'm getting," he groaned with something like pain. "The silk of your gown rubbing against me. Can you feel what you're doing to me?"

"Yes." She could barely get the word out. Her throat felt clogged, her lips felt as if they were on fire.

"I want you to feel more. *I* want to feel more."

He reached between them and drew her gown up over her hips. Lifting her up, he fitted her over him. She gasped in surprise, and he chuckled deep in his throat. "Oh, yes, my love. I *am* going to enjoy teaching you."

Ten

From the window in the large bedroom she now shared with Alex, Rachel could see the ceaseless flow of the river, northward to the Atlantic, a root beer-colored ribbon wending its way past her as it had most of her life. But things were different now. It had been several weeks since the day of her wedding, Rachel reflected, but still, she was having trouble adjusting to the idea of being Mrs. Alex Doral. When she spoke to Gran about it, Gran had said that an adjustment period was normal, that every young bride went through it. But Rachel had trouble believing that any other bride had ever tried to make a go of a marriage with the pressures she was under.

For one thing she couldn't seem to become accustomed to the luxuries with which Alex insisted on showering her.

Then there was the additional problem that

she never knew quite what to do with herself when Alex was busy working. Most days he spent long hours at the mill—she knew how important that was—and he still carried the responsibilities of his other businesses. But the upshot of it was that she was left home alone a great deal of the time without anything to do. Ruefully she remembered saying that was exactly what she wanted. But now that she had it, she found she hated it.

Carlos and the other servants ran the big house with the utmost efficiency, and she really had no desire to interfere with their routine. Alex had given her carte blanche to redecorate, but the exotic flavor of the house seemed exactly right for her husband, and she had no desire to change it. A lot of days she went to Gran's, but most of the work there had been finished, so there was very little for her to do over there either.

She had already taken Jaime shopping several times, indulging her sister in the beautiful clothes that Jaime had never had. The young girl seemed to take it all in stride, her energetic, sunny personality never changing. And Gran. Well, she didn't appear to need Rachel either. She had settled back into her newly refurbished house, her happiness evidenced by the new spring in her step and the light in her eyes. Her precious couch had been reupholstered, as had most of her other pieces; her treasures had been saved; and her beloved grand-daughter was happily married. Gran was obviously very happy, and for that Rachel was profoundly grateful.

And that brought her thoughts circling back to her marriage. Without coming right out and saying it, Rachel tried in every way she could to show Alex that she wanted their marriage to be a real one, based on love and not on what he could buy her. Even though he insisted that she sleep late, she always got up at the same time he did and had breakfast with him, sometimes even surprising him with breakfast in bed. Other times she would have Carlos drive her to the mill at the end of the day so that she could ride home with Alex.

But she could try only to show him, because somehow she could never quite bring herself to confess her love for him. She was too afraid he would reject her, and she knew she would never be able to stand that. And always their premarital agreement hung over her head like a sharp blade, reminding her of what a gold digger he must think her to be.

The only time she really relaxed was when she was in Alex's arms, and lately that didn't seem enough for her. She wanted more. She wanted his love.

"Are you ready?" Alex asked cheerfully, striding into the room. "We're leaving in fifteen minutes."

"Leaving? Where in the world are we going?"

"Didn't I tell you?" he asked innocently, while all the time his eyes were twinkling with playfulness. Before she married him, she would have never guessed this side of him existed, and although he didn't show it often, sometimes she got the impression that it surprised him almost as much as it did her.

Rachel's heart turned over with love. To see him like this, with no traces of hardness evident in his face, gave her hope for their marriage. "No, you know very well that you didn't. Now, where are we going and why are we going there in such a hurry?"

"New York." Alex casually called their destination over his shoulder as he disappeared into her closet. Reappearing moments later, he had one of the suits he had chosen for her before their marriage draped over his arm. "Just put this on. We're not taking any luggage. We'll buy everything we need when we get there."

"New York," Rachel repeated faintly. "I don't understand, Alex. *Why* are we going there?"

He tossed her suit on the bed and came to her. She saw that all playfulness had left his eyes, and in its place something very warm and mysterious had appeared. "Is there something wrong with a husband wanting to take his wife to New York on a second honeymoon?"

As always his closeness never failed to move her. She felt her heart skip a beat. "Second?"

"Well, our first has been right here, hasn't it?" She nodded as he gathered her into his arms with a smile. "And although there's been nothing wrong with it"—he paused to kiss her—"in fact, I've enjoyed it immensely, I've decided that a *second* honeymoon is in order. Okay?"

"Okay," she said softly.

"Good." He kissed her once again. "Now get dressed, because we have"—he consulted the gold watch on his wrist—"eight minutes before we have to leave."

They flew to New York in Alex's private jet, ensconced in the comfort and luxury of its custom-designed interior. En route they were served champagne by Carlos, who, Alex said, would be returning to Florida by commercial airliner. The jet, he explained, always stayed in the same city as he did, because he never knew when or where he would have to go next. It was a reminder of Alex's peripatetic life-style that Rachel didn't need. Would he ever be able to settle down in one place and be content? she wondered.

They landed in New York on a raw, cold afternoon. Just looking out the plane window at the gray day caused Rachel to shiver. She had done as Alex had bid and brought nothing but a small purse containing some cosmetics. Perhaps, she mused, she could find a lightweight cloth coat that would serve both to break the wind while she was in New York and still be suitable for the mild Florida winters.

Holding tightly to Alex's arm, she followed his lead as they made their way through the crowded terminal toward the exit, and she soon discovered they didn't have far to go. Waiting almost directly in front of the terminal was a gleaming black limousine with a smartly uniformed chauffeur.

"Good afternoon, Ronald," Alex greeted.

"Good afternoon, sir."

"Ronald, this is Mrs. Doral."

"Mrs. Doral." Ronald reached into the front seat of the car and brought out a full-length mink coat, handing it to Alex.

Alex held it out for her to slip into. "Rachel?"

"What?" she asked dazedly. It was the most beautiful coat she had ever seen, and he was holding it out for *her* to put on!

"It's for you. I knew you didn't have a suitable coat, so I ordered it for you. Let's see if it fits."

"Alex, I don't know what to say." Rachel found herself torn between her happiness that her husband had bought her such a beautiful gift, and the fact that every time he gave her something, she felt that much more cheapened. Not because she had married him for his money, but because he *thought* she had, and this was his way of buying her.

"It looks perfect on you," he murmured, pulling the fur collar up around her face, "and suddenly I can hardly wait to take it and everything else you're wearing off you. But right now we need to get to the apartment. New York is waiting."

The days and nights that followed were all Rachel could have wished for and more. Alex devoted himself to her exclusively, and she found that his complete attention was so potent, she could gladly bask in it. She had never been happier. In fact, she was so happy that she even accepted his gifts without too much protest. She didn't want to spoil this time they had together.

Their days were spent on sightseeing jaunts and on shopping trips so wildly extravagant, they left the sales personnel in the exclusive Fifth Avenue stores smiling broadly. The nights they spent checking out glamorous clubs, posh restaurants, and plays and musicals she had only read about.

But Rachel's favorite time was when they would arrive back at Alex's apartment late at night. High above the crowds, surrounded by the city's lights, Alex would take her in his arms, and the intensity that he showed never failed to astound her. It was as if it were the first time he had ever made love to her, and at the same time as if it were the last chance he would ever get.

Snow began to fall their last day in New York, and Alex bundled her into her mink for a carriage ride through Central Park. It was a memory to be stored up, Rachel told herself, for the time when there would be nothing left but memories.

Back in Cypress Cove their days settled into something of a routine. Alex's time was spent mostly at the mill, and Rachel decided to quit moping about. There was a lot of good she could do in her position as Alex's wife. She knew what it was like to be poor in Cypress Cove, so, she reasoned, what better than to associate herself with charities that helped the poor? As her first step she forced herself to become acquainted with the women, both young and old, who ran Cypress Cove society. She already knew them, of course, but as Rachel Kirkland. She had never felt she had much in common with these women—the wives and daughters of the town's leading businessmen—so she had never tried to become friends, considering herself an outcast.

But she decided to take the plunge all at once and invited them to tea. She found them to be eager to accept her invitation, but she had expected that. After all, she thought cynically, she was the wife of the man who had decided to give Cypress Cove and its residents a second chance.

For the most part Rachel found them to be all very cordial, even friendly, especially the young women her age. Only one note jarred, but to Rachel, who suffered from supersensitivity about her position, any nuance of a snub was enough to upset her. It came from a woman Rachel knew had reason to be particularly resentful of her because she had seen her throwing her marriageable-aged daughter in Alex's path a time or two in the weeks before their marriage.

The matron wiggled her wide hips into her seat cusion, as if she were preparing a nest for laying eggs, and said, "Aren't you fortunate to have married so well, dear? I mean, who would have thought it of little Rachel Kirkland? We all couldn't be happier for you."

There had been a definite condescending note in her voice, and Rachel's nails bit into the palms of her hands to keep them from shaking. Unknowingly the woman had hit upon what Rachel feared. She was convinced that everyone was silently thinking that she had married Alex for his money. Even Alex.

The woman's daughter, who had been homecoming queen in Rachel's senior year and was now a teacher in the local high school, smiled kindly at Rachel. "Don't mind Mother. She's just absolutely green with envy. She's never been able to reconcile having a daughter like me who, up to now, has not shown the slightest interest in marriage."

It made Rachel feel a little better, but still the matron's words stung. The afternoon had been a definite strain on her, and by the time it was over, her nerves felt positively strung out to the limit of their endurance.

As she saw the last of the ladies out the door, she bit her lip, angry that she had allowed herself to become so upset. She didn't want to let Alex see her in this mood, so she decided to take a long leisurely bath and try to soothe her bad mood away before he arrived home.

The bathroom, like the bedroom, had a marvelous view of the river, but Rachel was suddenly too tired to take advantage of it. She dropped a handful of bath salts into the marble tub, slowly submerged her body into the fragrant water, and surprisingly drifted off to sleep.

When she awoke, the water was cold, and Alex was standing before her, holding out a towel. "You'd better get out, before you get chilled and catch a cold."

"Oh, hi," she mumbled sleepily. "When did you get home?"

"Just a few minutes ago. I got home early and came to look for you and what did I find?" he teased gently. "My wife, the prune."

"Prune!" Rachel stood up immediately.

Alex laughed and wrapped a thick gold towel around her. "Don't worry, on you, wrinkles look magnificent."

Wrapping the towel sarong-fashion around herself, Rachel swept past him into the bedroom, secretly delighted by his teasing. "Alex, wrinkles look good only on elephants. And then only to other elephants."

"If you say so," he said, following her. "How did this afternoon go?"

Her good spirits plummeted. "Oh, all right, I guess. It's funny," she said, settling herself on the bed, "I've known those people most of my life, but I don't really know them. Do you know what I mean?"

"Oh, I think so. Having come to know you and that incredible defense system of yours, I would venture to say you never allowed yourself to know them." He came down beside her and began tugging at the towel.

"Alex!" She slapped his hand away only half playfully. She didn't want to make love to him now, with the confirmation of what the town thought of her so fresh in her mind. Funny, but she knew for certain that if she had married Sean, it wouldn't have mattered less to her. Alex was different, however. She loved Alex with all her heart.

He succeeded in wresting the towel away from her, then turned her so that they were lying side by side. And it was her love that made her resistance melt instantly at his touch. With the exception of his jacket, which he had tossed on a nearby chair, he was fully clothed.

Her lips brushed his and she began undoing the buttons of his shirt. "I missed you today," she whispered.

"Were the good ladies of Cypress Cove really that bad?" he asked in a husky voice Rachel now knew meant he wanted her. "You don't have to have anything to do with them, you know. You have only to please yourself—and me. . . ." He groaned as her hands pushed back his shirt and her tongue found one of his flat brown nipples.

"It's not that," she said softly, moving against him, wishing there were no clothes to separate them. "It's just that I miss you all the time when you're not here."

"Really?" He reached for the waistband of his pants and the fastener. "Oh, Rachel, I miss you too." Hungrily his mouth fastened on to hers, and his arms pulled her close; it was an hour later before either of them had a coherent thought.

When Rachel woke again, it was already dark outside. She stirred, and the tugging at her scalp told her that her hair had caught under Alex's shoulder. Extending a finger, she traced the outline of his lips with something like awe. She had shared so many intimacies with this man, yet she didn't feel secure with him and she certainly didn't feel she knew him.

Alex suppressed a smile. He loved holding Rachel within the circle of his arms like this after he had made love to her. It was one of his favorite times. There was no passion involved in this special time—just warmth and good feelings that lingered—and he wondered how he had ever existed without her and this time before. He opened his mouth and licked the tip of her finger.

"That's no fair," he heard Rachel protest. "You're awake."

He opened one eye, then closed it. "How can you tell?"

"Very funny." She repositioned her head on his shoulder.

"Have I told you lately how good you taste?" he asked.

"Yes."

"Well, then, have I told you lately how good you smell?"

"As a matter of fact, yes."

He could hear the smile in her voice, and it made him happy. If only she loved him as he did her, he would have everything he could ever wish for in life.

"Have I told you lately how wonderful you feel against me?"

"Yes."

If he could just keep her with him long enough, he thought, maybe she would forget that she had married him for his money and grow to love him.

"Have I told you lately that I have a gift for you?"

There was a pause. Then she said yes, but all the warm softness that Alex cherished so much had left her voice.

Alex opened his eyes and looked inquiringly at her. "What's wrong?"

She pressed her lips together and shook her head.

Alex had a very real feeling that something was wrong, but then he had had that feeling all afternoon. What could it be? Could she be hurting in some way and he didn't realize it? Could she be worried about something? Or could she simply be growing tired of him? He couldn't take the thought. He had to do something.

"Stay right where you are," he directed. Rising, he walked to where he had put down his briefcase. Snapping it open, he found what he was looking for—a small velvet jeweler's box. He turned back to her so that she could see it. "Since it seemed so important to you that you have only a gold wedding band, I held off getting you an engagement ring. But I saw this in New York and knew you had to have it."

Rachel froze. It was a large domed ring made of diamonds and yellow sapphires, brilliant and exquisite.

"The sapphires will pick up the gold in your eyes," he said casually, coming over to slip the ring on her lifeless finger.

It felt heavy and unfamiliar on her finger. Rachel stripped the ring off and handed it back to him. "How dare you!"

"What?"

"How dare you!" She jerked off the bed and snatched up the discarded towel. "I don't ever want you to give me another gift as long as you live, do you hear me? I'm tired of you buying me things, buying *me*." She could tell from the bewildered look on Alex's face that he had no idea what she was talking about. She wasn't sure she did either, but she couldn't stop. All she knew was that she couldn't bear it if he gave her another gift, especially now, after an afternoon of feeling that the whole town thought her a gold-digging bitch. And *especially* at this particular moment when her

body was still tingling from their wondrous love-making. To her it seemed only to underscore what Alex must think of her. "Just get out of here," she cried.

"All right, I will," he said coldly, "but if you don't mind, I'd just as soon get dressed first." He was watching her closely. "You know, if you didn't like the ring, all you had to do was say so. I can return it."

"Do that!" With the towel back in place, covering her, she hugged herself, completely miserable.

His tone changed, holding a hint of concern. "Rachel, are you feeling all right?"

"Of course," she answered sarcastically, pushing her fingers through her tousled hair. "Why wouldn't I be? After all, I have everything I've ever wanted."

"It's suddenly occurred to me that you've been taking a lot of naps lately."

"Well, maybe I'm just bored," she snapped. "Have you ever thought of that? Or maybe if you'd leave me alone once in a while"—she gestured toward the bed—"I wouldn't get so tired."

Alex looked at her for a long moment. "Dinner will be at seven as usual. If you don't feel like coming down, I'll have Carlos bring you up a tray."

He disappeared into his closet and reappeared a few minutes later dressed in a pair of black slacks and a blue shirt, then he left the room without a word.

Rachel collapsed back onto the bed, sobs tearing from her chest. What was she trying to do, she thought, drive him away before he was ready to go? She should be cherishing each moment that they had together instead of throwing a fit that would do any fishwife credit. She felt so ashamed.

She bathed her eyes in cold water until most of the ravages of her tears had disappeared. Then she took a quick, reviving shower. She didn't feel like dressing, so she put on one of her simpler at-home gowns—a long jade silk dress that wrapped around her narrow rib cage and tied on the side—and went down to try to apologize to Alex.

Her hand was on the doorknob of his study door when she heard his voice, loud, angry, incredulous.

"What? Are you sure? There's no mistake?"

Quietly opening the door, she could see Alex standing behind his desk, his ear to the receiver of the phone.

"All right, all right, now listen to me. Find out everything you can and then get back to me. I can't take any action until I have more information, so remember money is no object. . . . No, no. I'll deal with El León myself when and if the time comes."

He hung up the phone and slumped down into his chair.

"Alex, what's wrong?" She made her way around the desk until she was beside him. "Alex," she said again. "Who was that on the phone? What did they want?"

He spoke slowly. "It seems as if Rand has disappeared."

"Oh, no." She went down on her knees beside him. One of his hands was lying on the arm of the chair, balled tightly into a fist. She covered it with her hand.

"You know, all afternoon I had a feeling something was wrong," he said, "but I thought it was with you. That's why I came home early."

"What do you think has happened to him?"

"There could be only a couple of things," Alex

said grimly, "and neither of them are any good. Rand knows the country of Montaraz too well and has too much savvy to wander off and get lost. And most of the people of Montaraz think too highly of him to harm him, and that includes the guerrilla forces currently trying to topple El León's government. But there *is* a certain offshoot radical faction. I know their leader well. His name is Rafael, and he's a powder keg waiting to go off."

"What are you going to do? Contact the State Department?"

"No." He gave a brief laugh. "It would be too slow going through channels, and once I know what has happened, I can move in ways they would never sanction."

"You're not going down there, are you? Something could happen to you!" The thought of Alex risking his life nearly stopped her heart.

For the first time his eyes focused on her, and his lips curved upward gently. "Nothing's going to happen to me," he said quietly. "But I'm glad you care."

"I care. And Alex, I'm sorry about earlier." Weighed against the danger Rand was apparently in, her insecurities and problems seemed so petty. "I was on my way down to apologize when I heard you on the phone."

He threaded his long fingers through her hair and pulled her head against his chest. "There's no need for you ever to apologize, Rachel. Believe me, I know only too well how much you've had to adjust to since we married. I guess I wanted too much, too soon." His laugh was without humor. "It's the story of my life."

"What do you mean?"

He shook his head, the expression on his face

telling her that he was mocking himself. "Only that I've evidently been guilty of putting more pressure on you when I only wanted to lessen it."

She raised her head and kissed him, discovering that his concern and understanding for her in the face of his friend's plight only reinforced her love for him. "Why don't we agree that we're neither one to blame and start all over?"

"It's a deal." He glanced briefly at the phone. "It'll be hours before I hear anything. Let's go eat."

Alex made an effort during dinner to be his usual charming self, but it was obvious that he was worried. Afterward they retreated to the study and listened to music, but despite herself Rachel kept nodding off, and so with a tender kiss Alex sent her up to bed.

Eleven

Rachel wasn't sure what awakened her. At first everything seemed normal. The room was in darkness and Alex was beside her. She tried to think. Had it been a dream . . . or a sound? She twisted her head and looked at the illuminated dial on the bedside table. Three o'clock. She had been asleep about four hours. Glancing toward Alex, she wondered what time he had come to bed.

With a spontaneous action she reached her hand out to touch his arm. His skin felt damp, as if he were ill. And almost simultaneously as her mind registered that fact, she heard the moan and she knew that that was what had awakened her. It was a dreadful broken sound of someone in pain, *and it was coming from Alex*. Before she had time to react, he jerked his arm away from her and cried out, unintelligible words that were full of horror.

"Alex." Quickly she reached for the light.

"Alex," she repeated. But although the light was now on, he was still caught in the midst of his horrible dream. Unaware of her arms trying to subdue him, his sweating body thrashed about, and that terrible sound continued to tear from his throat.

"Alex!"

Suddenly two hard, bruising hands were gripping her shoulders. "No!" he yelled.

Hesitating only a moment, she began to slap his face lightly. She knew any pain she might cause him was nothing compared with the agony he was enduring in his sleep. But in one swift twisting move, she was pinned beneath his body. Staring down at her without recognition, his eyes were opened, and in them she could see a turbulent mixture of pain, hate, and . . . murder.

"Alex," she cried frantically, "it's me, Rachel."

Slowly his eyes focused. "Rachel?"

"Yes, darling. You were dreaming. Everything's all right now."

"Oh, my God." He shut his eyes for a moment, then opened them and looked at her. "Did I hurt you?"

"No, of course not. It was you I was worried about."

He rolled off her, onto his back, and flung his arm across his face. "I'm sorry," he said dully. "I hope I didn't frighten you."

She smoothed her hand across his chest, feeling the tremors that were still racking his body. "Alex, what happened?"

"Nothing," he denied. In an oddly vulnerable gesture he wrapped his arms across his chest and twisted away. "Nothing at all."

His voice had turned distant and formal, and Rachel knew it was his way of shutting her out. It hurt, but uppermost in her mind was that his body was still trembling in reaction to his nightmare. He was suffering, and she had to help him.

She settled herself back against the pillows, so that she was half lying, half sitting, then turned off the light and pulled the covers up over the two of them. Ignoring the fact that his back was to her and he was holding himself so stiffly, she slid up against him and put her arms around him.

"*Don't!* Just leave me alone."

A week ago—even an hour ago—if Alex had spoken that sharply to her, she would have gone scurrying out of the room, Rachel thought. But not now. Things had changed. She had caught a glimpse of the pain and mental anguish he had buried so deep, it only came out in his sleep, and all she could think about was trying to banish it.

"Be still," she murmured, holding his resisting body against her warmth, attempting to ease his cold and hurt away. She lost track of time as she whispered words of reassurance in the darkness and ran her hands over him as a mother would a hurt child, soothing him with her touch. It seemed a long time before she could feel him begin to relax. "Turn around," she urged softly.

Slowly, almost awkwardly, he turned until his head rested against her breast. "I'm sorry, Rachel," he whispered. "I thought the nightmares were a thing of the past. I would never have wanted to subject you to them."

"What happened?"

"It was the news of Rand's disappearance. It brought it all back."

"What? Tell me about the nightmares."

"They're of Montaraz . . . the jungles . . . the

firefights . . . the constant death and violence . . . man's inhumanity to man."

"That time of your life must have been horrible for you," she murmured.

"I wanted to help. I tried to help, but in the end it didn't matter. I fought for what I believed to be right, only to find out that it was wrong and that nothing I did mattered." He moved restlessly against her, but she stilled him, tightening her arms around him.

"That's not true. Rand once told me that you were the only one El León listened to, that things would be a lot worse today in Montaraz if it hadn't been for your urging of temperance. You saved lives."

"I also killed."

"To save lives."

"Somehow that doesn't sound right, does it?" he murmured sadly. "There's a day that keeps recurring in my dreams . . . a day I can't forget. I was leading a team of guerrillas on a routine patrol when we came under fire from a small squad of government troops. We were positioned across a clearing from one another, and this child—this tiny little boy, who couldn't have been more than four years old—wandered into the clearing. I immediately called a cease-fire, but the government troops kept firing. They cut him down, and over the gunfire came the sound of his mother's screams."

"I don't understand," Rachel exclaimed with horror. "What was the child doing there?"

"Who knows? There was a village nearby where I'm sure he and his family were living. He had probably played in that clearing many times before the revolution. He was just one of those casualties that rarely get reported back in the States, a victim caught up in something that wasn't his fault. I lost a little of my mind that day. Maybe even a little of my soul. I charged across that clearing and single-handedly killed every government soldier there. I should have been killed. As a matter of fact, I remember praying that I would be. But luck and rage were on my side."

His tears covered her breast and gown by the time he finished speaking. "Stop it," she ordered softly, and held him even tighter. "Stop blaming yourself. You did what you thought you had to do, but it's over. You're here with me now. You're safe."

"But where is Rand?" Alex asked.

Rachel had no answer. So she held Alex tightly through the night, cradling him in her arms while he dozed fitfully. And in the darkness she remembered what Rand had told her. *The scars heal over and are replaced by needs that maybe only another scarred person can fill.* She knew now that Alex indeed had scars, but she had to ask herself if she could help him. Would he *let* her help him? There were no answers, but the answer to where Rand was came the next morning.

Alex slammed down the receiver of the phone. "It's as I feared. They're holding Rand for ransom."

"Oh, no!" Rachel sank into the chair opposite his desk. "What will happen to him?"

"Nothing, if I can help it," Alex said grimly. "I'm going in after him."

Cold terror flooded through her at the thought of Alex putting himself in danger. "*No!* You can't. I won't let you."

"I'm the only one who can, Rachel," he said quietly.

God knew, he didn't want to go back to

Montaraz, he thought, watching Rachel rise and pace to the fireplace. And he sure as hell didn't want to leave Rachel—not now, when it looked as if she were drawing closer to him.

Last night he had relived the hell he had been trying to forget ever since he had left Montaraz, the country that was the source of most of his demons. And reliving it had only been bearable because of Rachel. His first reaction when he had awakened from the nightmare had been his usual—to close himself off and suffer alone. But she hadn't let him. She had gotten through his guard and he had found himself talking with her about it, sharing a little of the hell that had been his alone for so many years. And miracle of miracles, somehow she had understood and made it a little easier.

He hadn't thought it was possible, but his love for her had grown during the night that had just passed. Leaving her would be one of the hardest things he had ever had to do—he would have to steel himself to do it—but he had to go. Rand was the one person on earth he would revisit that hell for.

Her voice broke through his thoughts. "What about your responsibilities, Alex? You can't just up and take off."

"My friend is my responsibility, Rachel."

She felt all the air go out of her. What was she doing, telling Alex not to go after Rand? Rand was in danger, and she knew the man whom she had come to love would never leave his friend to die in a jungle far away from home. Not when there was a chance he could help save him.

"I'm sorry, Alex. Of course, you have to go. I'm just frightened for your safety."

"I don't want you to worry," he said softly.

"Years of being away from the life of a mercenary haven't softened me that much. All my instincts of survival are still firmly in place. And I have friends, men who fought beside me, still there who will help me."

She had a thought. "Can I go with you?"

"Absolutely not! I'll be traveling very fast and with the utmost secrecy. It'll be my only chance . . . and Rand's."

Seeing her disheartened expression, Alex got up and walked around the desk to her. He took her face between his hands. "I need to know you'll be right here, safe, waiting for me. Will you do that for me?"

"Yes," she said softly. "I'll do that for you."

Once Alex made his decision to go, time moved very quickly. It seemed to Rachel that she had hardly drawn a breath before Alex was saying good-bye to her. Dressed in jungle camouflage, he seemed a stranger. And he spoke like one too.

"Rachel, I've asked Carlos to make you a doctor's appointment. I don't like the way you've been looking lately. Promise me you'll go."

At this moment she would have promised him anything. "All right. And you promise me something."

"What's that?"

There was a strange expression in his eyes. Why was he standing so far away from her, she wondered, when she needed to feel his arms around her one more time before he left? "You come back."

Alex hated himself before he even said it, but the last days of worrying about Rand and his own uncertainties over his relationship with Rachel had gotten the better of him. He couldn't even bear to take her in his arms for fear he wouldn't be able to let her go. "Count on it," he said gruffly. "But don't be sad. If I don't, you'll have my money to console you."

She hadn't been ready for the attack. "What?" she asked, shocked.

"Surely you've memorized our premarital agreement, if not framed it. If I die, you get everything."

Carlos walked quietly into the room. "The car is waiting, Señor Alex."

"I'll be right there." He looked back at Rachel, regretting that they were parting in this way, but there was no time left. His damn demons. Would they never leave him? His lips dropped to hers with a quick bruising pressure. "Good-bye, Rachel," he said, and walked out.

He hadn't even given her time to say good-bye to him, she thought dazedly, not at all sure what had just happened between them. "Damn him," she said softly to no one at all. "Damn him."

With Alex gone the days seemed to creep on feet of fear and anxiety. There was no word, and he had told her very little of his plans. She only knew he was flying his jet into San José, the capital of Costa Rica. And from there he would take a helicopter into the interior of Montaraz to a place he considered a safe landing area. But would it be? she asked herself over and over. What if this Rafael had an ambush planned? What if Alex were lying wounded on the jungle floor somewhere? Or worse, what if he were dead?

Rachel was frantic with worry. Then, the more she worried, the madder she got. Why had he made that crack about their premarital agreement? And what was he doing risking his life, when she loved him so much?

And then she got mad at herself. Why on earth hadn't she told him that she loved him? Why had she let him go off on a dangerous mission without telling him? She called herself every name in the book. And then she would get mad at Alex again.

It wasn't rational, she freely admitted to herself, but she didn't care. All she wanted was Alex back in her arms.

And so it went, with each day more unbearable than the last. The morning Carlos came to remind her of her doctor's appointment, he found her crying.

"Please do not distress yourself, señora. I fought alongside Señor Alex in Montaraz. And never was there a man so brave or so strong. Señor Alex will come home safely."

"I know he will," she said, attempting to brush away the traces of her tears with trembling fingers. "And by the way cancel my doctor's appointment. I don't want to go."

"Señora," Carlos said, his manner courteous yet firm. "Señor Alex made a special request that I see you to the doctor's. I plan to see you to the doctor's."

A little shocked because Carlos was usually so retiring, Rachel raised her eyebrows in question.

"Señora," he continued, his voice gentler, "the scar on Señor Alex's face was received when he saved me from enemy fire so treacherous, a normal man would have had trouble saving himself, much less another man. But he saved my life. And he told me to take care of you. I plan to take care of you."

She sighed, giving in. "All right, Carlos, we'll

go to the doctor." She probably did need to go, she thought wearily. If for nothing else than to straighten out the mess she had made of her birth control-pill schedule.

An hour later, after her doctor had examined her, Rachel was telling him about it. "Somehow I can never seem to remember to take them."

The doctor didn't even blink. "Which is precisely why you are now pregnant, Rachel."

"I'm *what*?" she exclaimed, and burst out crying.

"Pregnant," the doctor said matter-of-factly, and handed her a Kleenex. "Which explains the frequent naps you've been taking and the mood swings you've been telling me about. Don't be alarmed by them, by the way. It's all completely normal. At this time in your life you'll probably find yourself crying over Hallmark-card commercials on TV."

Rachel blew her nose. "And all this time I thought the reason was Alex."

"Well, I think he can take at least half the blame," the doctor said, his eyes sparkling with an entirely different meaning.

Alex arrived back in the States seven days after he had left it, exhausted, but satisfied with a job well done. Rand needed minor medical attention, so at his insistence Alex had dropped him off in Houston before continuing on to Cypress Cove.

He landed at six o'clock in the afternoon, impatient to see Rachel. But the minute he walked through the front door, he knew something was wrong. Rachel was not waiting for him. Searching the downstairs first, he couldn't find her. He bounded up the stairway, calling her name as he went, a terrible unease gripping him.

Rachel heard Alex call her name and tensed. These last seven days she had been living to see him again, but now that he was here, she was scared to death. Time after time this past week, she had had to remind herself that Alex was not David, and that he would not react the way David had when she had told him she was pregnant. Alex had said he wanted children. He wouldn't desert her. He had a strength of character that David had never had.

Maybe their marriage hadn't turned out as Alex had planned, but Rachel was convinced they could make it work. Even if he didn't love her, she prayed he would love their child. The main thing, she told herself, was not to choke up. From somewhere within herself, she had to find the courage to talk to Alex, openly and honestly, because the next few minutes might well decide the rest of her life—and her baby's.

Alex burst through the door and stopped. Rachel was reclining on a chaise longue, wearing a gold robe, and her chestnut hair was in loose, disorderly curls about her shoulders as if she had been running her hand through it. She looked beautiful, and the deep relief he felt on seeing her safe and well almost made him weak.

"Rachel, why weren't you downstairs or at the airport waiting for me? I cabled ahead."

She nervously fingered the folds of her robe, all the while thinking how much she wanted to run to him and throw her arms around him. "I wanted to talk to you alone, without other people around."

She sounded so serious, Alex noted with a sinking feeling in his stomach. In the past seven days he had faced deadly guerrillas with less dread than he suddenly felt facing her now.

Rachel's emotions regarding Alex reminded her of the time she saw a mother jerk her child from in front of a car and proceed to alternately spank and hug the child, so mad was the mother that the child had endangered his life, and so thankful was she that her child was all right.

But this was no child standing in front of her. This was her husband. "I'm glad you're home," she said softly.

He started toward her. "Rachel."

She held up a hand. "No, stay where you are. I—I won't be able to tell you the things I need to tell you if you're close."

"For God's sake, Rachel. What is it?"

"Well . . . I guess that our premarital contract is a good place to start."

"Premarital contract!" he exploded in disbelief. "Am I hearing right? For seven days I've been crawling through a steaming jungle, existing on very little except the thought of getting back to you, and now that I'm back, you won't let me near you until we talk about our premarital contract?"

She nodded, nearly losing her courage.

He drew a cheroot out of his pocket and stuck it between his teeth. "What is it you want added to the contract, Rachel?"

It was his hard, cynical tone that gave her courage back to her. "Nothing at all, Alex. But that's typical of you to assume I do. Actually I want it torn up. I never wanted it in the first place."

In the act of lighting the cheroot, he lifted his head and looked at her oddly. "Rachel, that document was for your protection, to give you peace of mind."

"Peace of mind!" She jumped to her feet. "How can one man be so dumb?"

A faint hope begin to flicker in the back of Alex's brain, but before he could respond, she rushed on.

"And another thing, you're going to have to stop smoking."

"My smoking never bothered you before."

"I know," she said nervously. "It's just one of the symptoms."

"Symptoms? Rachel, are you all right?"

"No, of course, I'm not all right. I haven't been all right since you left. Which reminds me. The next thing you need to know is that I understand why you had to go after Rand. But"—she looked at him, then turned away, deciding she might feel braver if she couldn't see his hard face—"you will leave me again over my dead body."

The flicker of hope was burning brightly now. "Rachel, what are you trying to say?"

"I'm not *trying* to say anything. I'm saying it. Aren't you listening?" She swung around, only to find that he had moved closer to her.

"God knows, I'm trying, but you're not making a lot of sense."

"That's just another symptom." She waved her hand dismissively. "The main thing to remember is, no more dangerous missions. I am personally going to see to it that Rand will never go back to Montaraz again. And—"

"I've just got to ask," he interrupted, a touch of humor creeping into his voice, "how you're going to prevent Rand from going back to Montaraz."

"I'll get to that. Now, where was I?"

"I think you were trying to tell me something," he said gently.

"You're right, I am. I don't ever want you to put your life in danger again." She licked her lips nervously. That wasn't what she had meant to say, but his energy was filling the room, making it hard to concentrate. "And I hated the cutting remark you threw at me about the premarital agreement right before you walked out the door seven days ago."

By now he was standing directly in front of her. "I'm sorry if I hurt you, Rachel. It was inexcusable of me, but I was hurting too. Leaving you was the last thing I wanted to do."

"Really?" She felt so vulnerable, she thought. Could she let herself believe that he might return her feelings of love?

He nodded. "Really. Now, are you sure that's all you want to say? Isn't there something else?"

"All right," she murmured, knowing it was now or never. "There is something else that you need to know. *I love you.* And I want our marriage to be a real one in every sense of the word. And I want to have your children. And I never want you to leave me again. Now are you satisfied?"

"Yes," he said, scooping her up in his arms and carrying her to the bed. "Oh, yes. Because my darling Rachel, I love you too. I didn't even know love existed until I met you and now I'll never let you go."

A long time later Alex murmured, "I have to ask. How are you going to keep Rand from returning to Montaraz?"

"Oh, that's easy. I'm going to give him the responsibility of being a godfather."

Alex smiled tenderly. "To be a godfather we're going to have to give him a godchild."

"It's been taken care of. He'll only have to wait six and a half months."

"*Rachel!*"

THE EDITOR'S CORNER

Next month should be called "Especially Fabulous Reading Month!" Not only is Bantam publishing four marvelous LOVESWEPTS (of course) and Sandra Brown's sensational sequel to **SUNSET EMBRACE, ANOTHER DAWN,** but also we are reissuing Celeste DeBlasis's extraordinary novel, **THE PROUD BREED.**

An excerpt from ANOTHER DAWN follows this Editor's Corner; next month you can look forward to an excerpt from **THE PROUD BREED.** I know you're going to enjoy both of these longer novels very, very much. By the way, some booksellers display books like **ANOTHER DAWN** and **THE PROUD BREED** in general fiction or in special displays in areas of their stores where you might not think to look for them. So, if you don't see these novels right away, do make a special point of asking your bookseller for them.

Now for those Fabulous Four LOVESWEPTS coming next month.

Sara Orwig creates for all of us a mellow, yet thrilling romance, **DEAR MIT,** LOVESWEPT #111. Just think of the nostalgic pleasure of receiving a letter from your very best friend (and very best tormentor) throughout childhood with whom you've lost touch. Then add that in the present that friend is a thoroughly adult male and a very amusing correspondent who hasn't forgotten a thing about you. Now you're ready to put yourself in heroine Marilyn Pearson's place and imagine her response when at last she encounters Colly face-to-face and finds him devastatingly attractive. And the feeling is definitely mutual. "Mellow," "nostalgic," or any other kind of tame emotion flies right out the window then and it's all sparks and fire between them. But their lives have developed along diverse paths and seem impossible to meld—except perhaps when they stand together beneath the old

(continued)

pear tree that was their special childhood spot. . . . Well, we'll keep you guessing about what happens there, but we won't keep you in suspense about our feeling that **DEAR MIT** is one of Sara's most original, funny, and endearing romances ever!

Given your wonderfully warm welcome for Peggy Webb's first romance, **TAMING MAGGIE,** LOVE-SWEPT #106, I know you'll be very pleased to learn that she has another book coming up next month, **BIRDS OF A FEATHER,** LOVESWEPT #112. In this delectable story, young widow Mary Ann Gilcrest finds herself—much to her dismay and her mother's delight—in the midst of a birdwatchers' retreat. But suddenly it isn't such a dismal event; as a matter of fact it becomes a downright wonderful one! And the not-so-simple reason for the change in Mary Ann's view is magnificent Bill Benson. Alas, their days together in the wilderness are over much too soon and they must go their separate ways. Then Bill promises forever, but she can't believe in their future together. Bill's relentless pursuit causes a furor to break out in her hometown . . . and the most charming madness surrounds this wonderful couple in an ending to **BIRDS OF A FEATHER** that you aren't likely to forget!

And next we have a sensitive, most imaginative author joining us, Linda Hampton, with **A MATTER OF MAGIC,** LOVESWEPT #113. Linda's delightful debut book with LOVESWEPT features the most romantic sleight-of-hand from a marvelous hero, Murray Richards. How he impresses heroine Georgette Finlay when he helps her retrieve a pile of dropped packages and then produces a rose from thin air! Georgette feels it is truly providential that they met because she's a talent agent who's been scouting long and hard for a magician. She does a hard sell job on Murray—but he isn't buying! Magic is strictly a hobby for the high-powered executive. No, he wants a far different relationship with Georgette . . . but will he pull it off only by using every trick of the illusionist's trade to weave a spell of sensual enchantment around her? Getting the answer to that question is getting a sure-fire treat in romantic reading!

Be sure to have a box of tissues nearby when you pick up Joan Elliott Pickart's **RAINBOW'S ANGEL**, **LOVESWEPT #114**, because this lovely story is probably going to bring tears of sentiment and laughter to your eyes. The hero is the debonair R. J. Jenkins from **SUNLIGHT'S PROMISE** and from the moment he lays eyes on Kelly Morgan he's a goner! Their first encounter takes his breath away . . . their next meeting impresses him with her business acumen . . . their third meeting melts his heart. Kelly touches R. J. as no woman ever has with her beauty, brains, courage, and heart. But they have so little time together and R. J. has to make many difficult decisions before he can commit to Kelly, the adoring mother of toddler Sara. **RAINBOW'S ANGEL** is one of Joan's most touching, truly emotional love stories.

We hope you'll agree with us that the four LOVE-SWEPTs along with **ANOTHER DAWN** and **THE PROUD BREED** add up to "Especially Fabulous Reading Month" from Bantam Books.

With every warm wish,

Sincerely,

Carolyn Nichols

Carolyn Nichols
  Editor
LOVESWEPT
Bantam Books, Inc.
666 Fifth Avenue
New York, NY 10103

Jake followed Banner into the living room. He trod lightly, like a convict who had just been granted a stay of execution. She seemed tranquil enough, but he didn't trust her mood. He had meddled in her business when she had made it plain his interference into her personal life was unwelcome. If she wanted to dally with Randy, who was he to stop her?

Then he had kissed her. What had possessed him to kiss her like that this afternoon? He had been mad enough to strangle her, but he had sought another outlet for his emotions, one even more damaging. He wouldn't have been surprised if she had opened fire on him the minute he drove into the yard. Instead she was treating him like a king just returned to the castle.

"Hang your hat on the rack, Jake," she said. "And I don't think you'll need that gunbelt any more tonight."

"Banner, about this afternoon—"

"Never mind about that."

"Let me apologize."

"If you must, apologize to Randy. He hadn't done anything to warrant you pulling a gun on him."

"I intend to apologize to him tomorrow. I don't know what got into me." He spread his hands wide in a helpless gesture. "It's just that Ross told me to protect you, and when I heard you screaming—"

"I understand."

"And about the other—"

"Are you sorry you kissed me, Jake?"

Her face commanded all his attention. It shone pale and creamy in the golden lamplight, surrounded by the dark cloud of her hair. Her eyes were wide with inquiry, as though how he answered her question was of the utmost importance. Her lips were as tremulous and moist as if he had just kissed them.

His answer was no. But he couldn't admit it out loud, so he said nothing. He had behaved like a man possessed this afternoon when he saw Randy's hands on Banner. She was obviously jealous of Priscilla. Jealousy between them was dangerous. And he knew it. And the sooner he called an end to this cozy evening, the better. "I need to be getting—"

"No, wait." She took two rapid steps forward. When he looked at her as though she had taken leave of her senses, she fell back a step. Catching her hands at her waist, she said quickly, "I have a favor to ask. If you . . . if you have the time."

"What is it?"

"In the living room. I have a picture to hang and I wondered if you could help me with it."

He glanced over his shoulder toward the center room. One small lamp was burning in the corner. The room was cast in shadows, as intimate as those in the barn had been. The parlor was also the scene of the kiss that afternoon. Jake was better off not being reminded of that at all.

"I'm not much good at picture hanging," he hedged.

"Oh, well." She made a dismissive little wave with her hand. "You've put in a full day already and it isn't the foreman's job to hang pictures, I suppose."

Hell. Now she thought he didn't want to help her. She looked crestfallen, disappointed that she wouldn't get her picture hung and embarrassed for having asked his help and being turned down.

"I guess it wouldn't take too long, would it?"

"No, no," she said, lifting her head eagerly. "I have everything ready." She brushed past him on her way into the parlor. "I got the hammer and a nail from the barn this afternoon while you were gone. I tried to hang it myself, but couldn't tell if I was getting it in the right spot or not."

She was chattering breathlessly. Jake thought she might be as nervous as he about returning to this room. But she made no effort to turn up the lamp or light another one. Instead she made a beeline for the far wall.

Was this her way of telling him that she had forgiven his behavior that afternoon, that she wasn't afraid to be in an empty house with him long after the sun had gone down? Had everything she had done tonight been a peacemaking gesture? If so, he was grateful to her. They couldn't have gone on much longer without killing each other or . . .

The "or" he would do well not to think about. Especially since she was facing him again.

"I thought I'd hang it on this wall, about here," she said, pointing her finger and cocking her head to one side.

"That would be nice." He felt about as qualified to give advice on hanging a picture as he would be to choose a chapeau in a milliner's shop.

"About eye level?"

"Whose eye level? Yours or mine?"

She laughed. "I see what you mean." She scraped the top of her head with her palm and slid it horizontally until it bumped against his breastbone. "I only come to here on you, don't I?"

When she glanced up at him, his breath caught somewhere between his lungs and his throat. How could he have ever considered this creature with the bewitching eyes and teasing smile a child? He had been with whores who prided themselves on knowing all there was to know about getting a man's blood to the boiling point. But no woman had ever had an impact on him the way this one did. Except perhaps Lydia those months they were together on the wagon train.

His love for her had mellowed since then. He no longer experienced rushes of passionate desire every time he saw her. That summer traveling between Tennessee and Texas, he had been perpetually randy. Desire for Lydia, desire for Priscilla, desire for women, period.

He had been sixteen, the sap of youth flowing sweetly, but painfully, through his body. But that's what he felt like every time he looked at Banner. He felt sixteen again and with no more control over his body than he had then.

Her skirt was rustling against his pants. Her breasts were achingly close to his chest. She smelled too good for it to be legal. He could practically taste her breath as it softly struck his chin. Before he drowned in the swirling depths of her eyes, he said, "Maybe we'd better—"

"Oh, yes," she said briskly. Taking a three-legged stool from in front of an easy chair, she placed it near the wall and, raising her skirt above her ankles, stepped up on it. "The picture is there on the table. Hand it to me, please, then step back and tell me when it looks right."

He picked up the framed picture. "This is pretty."

It was a pastoral scene of horses grazing in a verdant pasture. "I thought it looked like Plum Creek." She glared at him, daring him to say anything derogatory about the name she had selected.

"I didn't say anything."

"No, but I know what you're thinking," she said accusingly. He only smiled benignly and passed her the picture.

She turned her back, raised her arms and positioned the picture. "How does that look?"

"A little lower maybe."

"There?"

"That's about right."

Keeping the picture flat against the wall, she craned her head around. "Are you really judging or are you just trying to get this over with?"

"I'm doing the best I can," he said, acting offended. "If you don't appreciate my help, you can always ask somebody else."

"Like Randy?"

Her taunt was intended as a joke, but Jake took it seriously. His brows gathered into a V above his nose as he took in the picture *she* made perched on that stool, leaning toward the wall with her arms raised. There was a good two inches of lacy petticoat showing above her trim ankles. Her rear end was sticking out. The apron's bow, topping that cute rounded bottom, was a tease no man could resist. The way her breasts poked out in front clearly defined their shape. No, not Randy. Not anybody if Jake could help it.

He considered the placement of the picture with more care this time. "A little to the left if you want it centered." She moved it accordingly. "There. That's perfect."

"All right. The nail will have to go in about six inches higher because of the cord it hangs by. Bring it and the hammer. You can drive it in while I hold the frame."

He did as he was told, straddling the stool and leaning around her. He tried to avoid touching her, adjusting his arms in several positions, none of them satisfactory.

"Just reach up between my arms with one hand and go over the top with the other."

He swallowed and held his breath, trying not to notice her breasts as his hand snaked up between them. He held the nail in place with the other, though that was no small task because he was shaking on the inside.

This was ridiculous! How many woman had he tumbled? Stop acting like a goddamn kid and just get the job done so you can get the hell out of here! he shouted inwardly.

Carefully he drew the hand holding the hammer back. But not carefully enough. His elbow pressed against her side. One of his knees bumped the back of hers. The backs of his knuckles sank into the plumpness of her breasts.

"Excuse me," he muttered.

"That's all right."

He struck the nail, praying it would go into the wall

with only one blow. It didn't. He moved his hand back and struck it again, and again, until he could see progress. Then, in rapid succession, he hit it viciously several times.

"That's good enough," he said gruffly, and withdrew his arms.

"Yes, I think so." Her voice sounded as unsteady as his.

She draped the silken cord around the head of the nail and leaned as far back as she could while still maintaining her balance on the stool.

"How's that?"

"Fine, fine." He laid the hammer on the nearest table and ran his sleeve over his perspiring forehead.

"Is it straight?"

"A little lower on the left."

"There?"

"Not quite."

"There?"

Damn, he cursed silently. He had to get out of here or he was going to explode. He strode forward, wanting to straighten the picture quickly so he could leave and get some much needed air to clear his head. But in his haste, the toe of his boot caught on one of the stool's three legs and it rocked perilously.

Banner squeaked in alarm and flailed her arms.

Life on the trail for so many years had given Jake reflexes as quick as summer lightning. His arms went around her faster than the blink of an eye and anchored her against him. When the stool clattered onto its side, Banner was being held several inches off the floor.

One of Jake's arms was around her waist, the other hand was flattened against her chest. Rather than letting her slide down, he lowered her. His back rounded slightly as he followed her down, bending over her.

But once her feet were safely on the floor, he didn't release her. Jake had spread his legs wide to break her fall. Now Banner's hips were tucked snugly in the notch between his thighs.

His cheek was lying along hers and when her nearness and her warmth and her scent got to be too much for him to resist, he turned his head and nuzzled her ear with his nose. His arms automatically tightened around her. He groaned her name.

How could anything that felt so right be so wrong? Lord, he wanted her. Knowing in his deepest self that what had happened that other time was an abomination against decency, he wanted her again. There was no use lying to himself that he didn't. He had hurt her once. He had sworn never to again. He had betrayed a friendship that meant more to him than anything in the world.

Yet such arguments were burned away like fog in a noonday sun as his lips moved in her hair and his nose breathed in the fragrance of the cologne that had been dabbed on that softest of spots behind her ear.

"Banner, tell me to leave you alone."

"I can't."

She moved her head to one side, giving him access. His lips touched her neck.

"Don't let this happen again."

"I want you to hold me."

"I want to, I want to."

He moved his hand from her chest up to her neck, then her chin, until his hand lightly covered her face. Through parted lips her breath was hot and quick on his palm.

Like a blind man, he charted each feature of her face with calloused fingertips suddenly sensitized to capture each nuance. He smoothed her brows, which he knew to be raven black and beautifully arched. His fingers coasted over her cheekbones. They were freckled. He had come to adore every single freckle. Her nose was perfect, if a bit impudent.

Her mouth.

His fingers brushed back and forth over her lips. They were incredibly soft. The warm breaths filtering through them left his fingers moist.

He pressed his mouth to her cheek, her ear, into her hair.

The hand at her waist opened wide over her midriff. He curled his fingers against the taut flesh. She whimpered. He argued with himself, but there was no stopping his hand from gliding up the corrugated perfection of her ribs and covering her breast. Their moans complemented each other.

Her ripe fullness filled his hand, and against his revolving thumb, the center of her breast tightened into a bead of arousal.

"Jake—"

"Sweet, so sweet."

"This happens sometimes."

"What?"

"That," she answered on a puff of air as his fingers closed around her nipple. "They get that way sometimes . . . when I look at you."

"Good God, Banner, don't tell me that."

"What does it mean?"

"It means I never should have stayed."

"And they won't go down. Not for the longest time. They stay like that, kind of itchy and tingling—"

"Oh, hush."

"—and that's when I wish—"

"What?"

"—that we were in the barn again and you were—"

"Don't say it."

"—inside me."

"Jesus, Banner, stop."

He made a cradle of his palm and laid it along her cheek, gradually turning her head to face him. And as her head turned, so did her body. The fabric of her clothes dragged against his like the tide on the seashore, separate, yet bound.

When their eyes met and locked hungrily, he lowered his mouth to hers. He thrust his tongue deep into her mouth as he pressed her hips against him.

He tore his mouth free. "No, Banner. I hurt you before, remember?"

"Yes, but that wasn't why I was crying."

"Then why?"

"Because it began to feel good and I . . . I thought you'd hate me for the way I was acting."

"No, no," he whispered fervently into her hair.

"You were so . . . big."

"I'm sorry."

"I just didn't expect it to be so . . . and . . . and so . . ."

"Did it feel good to you at all, Banner?"

"Yes, yes. But it was over too soon."

He laid his hard cheek against hers. His breathing was labored, otherwise he didn't move. "Too soon?"

"I felt like something was about to happen, but it didn't."

Jake was stunned. Could it be? He knew whores faked it. He didn't have any experience with decent women. Certainly not with virgins. Never with a virgin. He had never taken anyone he could feel tenderness for.

But tenderness for Banner enveloped him now. He cupped her face between his hands and went searching in her eyes for the truth. He saw no fear there, only a keen desire that matched his own. Making a growling sound deep in his throat, he lowered his head again.

"Hello!" a cheerful voice called out. "Anyone at home?"

Only then did they become aware of the jingle of harnesses and the unmistakable sounds of a wagon being pulled to a halt outside.

"Banner? Where are you?"

It was Lydia.

LOVESWEPT

Love Stories you'll never forget by authors you'll always remember

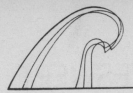

LOVESWEPT

Love Stories you'll never forget by authors you'll always remember